Ladybug

Maggie Leith Stone

Ladybug

by Maggie Ruth Stone

S

MAGGIE RUTH STONE MINISTRIES
Nashville, Tennessee

Design/Typesetting/Production by SCHATZ+SCHATZ, Nashville

Published in Nashville, Tennessee, by Maggie Ruth Stone Ministries, 1991.

Printed in the United States of America.

ISBN 0-9627059-3-4

*This book
is lovingly dedicated
to my husband
"Stoney"
without whose love
this book
might never
have been written.*

*It is also dedicated
to my wonderful doctor
and friend,
Dr. Louis Rosenfeld,
who took care of me
so very well
when I had
the same operation
as Jeanine.*

About the Author

"Maggie" Ruth Stone, beloved grandmother and storyteller, has written over 25 Christian romance novels. These stories have grown out of her desire to give her five granddaughters a Christian view of love and romance.

Ruth Stone and her husband, Harlan, have one daughter, Leslie and two sons, John and Paul. They lived previously in Hazard, Kentucky, where Harlan was the band director at the local high school. A new job took them to Nashville, Tennessee.

For the past 25 years Maggie Ruth has served as secretary to the head of the transportation division of the Metro School System. She is a living miracle of God's healing power experienced in a battle with cancer. She shares all she learned through that time in her gracious care and concern for other's suffering.

For the past four years, Maggie Ruth has written a weekly column entitled, "A Letter From Aunt Maggie," which appears in two community newspapers, reaching 50,000 people. It is a column about life, love and happiness, as told in quotations from other people, her own philosophy and the Bible. At the end of each "Aunt Maggie" column, she exhorts her readers to maintain a positive attitude. "Take care," she writes, "and keep looking up." This advice has obviously worked for Maggie Ruth Stone.

Published Titles by the Author

Casa Valledorres (A Trilogy)
The Portrait (Part I)
Branded (Part II)
Camden (Part III)

Unpublished Titles by the Author

The House on Maple Street
To Fetch a Pail of Laughter
The Face in the Mirror
The Shadow of a Smile
Chrissy
The Beckoning Willows
Shara's Dream
Tiffany's Choice
Trouble on Troublesome
Miss Molly's Web
Pink Lady
Little Suzie
Her Foolish Heart
The Quest
The Tamberlanes
A Picture, Torn
Garron's Dilemma
Tug of Hearts
Canfield Connection
A Love Remembered

For information regarding these titles, write to:
Maggie Ruth Stone Ministries
76 Tusculum Road
Antioch, Tennessee 37013

Chapter 1

"Drat that man! Oh, drat that man! He makes me so angry. What wouldn't I like to say to him if I had half a chance!" Jeanine Page threw the newspaper down on the sofa next to her beautiful sister, shaking her short black curls.

"Well, why don't you?" Jan asked.

"Why don't I what?"

"Write him. You're always writing letters to the editor about something or other. Why don't you write to him?"

"It wouldn't do any good. He writes like he's a humanist and you can't convince them of anything. What makes me so angry is that they seem to have grafted themselves into every part of our government. They are in entertainment, in our public schools, in the papers and TV and even our economic system." Jeanine's temper was still showing as she got up and paced in front of her sister, her short tan legs and petite figure more like a slender teenage boy than the twenty-four year old she was. In her khaki shorts and glistening white, short sleeved blouse she looked like a sports woman for sure. The open collar and short sleeves showed neck and arms glowing with well-tanned health and vitality from her long stints of sailing in the sun on the Cumberland River flowing below their hilltop home near Nashville, Tennessee.

"Well, what is a humanist anyway?" Jan's blue eyes and black page boy were such an arresting combination Jeanine thought enviously as she looked at her sister.

"A humanist is someone who thinks that man and only man is the answer to all man's problems. They make no reference to God or the Bible. In fact, they think they can ignore God and get away with it. The worst part is that Dr. Ben is a very intelligent person. How could he be a doctor and not be intelligent, but it makes me angry to see that kind of intelligence wasted. If only he could see the fallacy of his beliefs." She raised her two small fists and shook them in the air.

"What kind of doctor is he?"

"Just a regular doctor I guess, but that's just it. He of all people should know better. He can't heal people. He's just a vessel in God's hands and with God to guide him think how much more effective he would be. If only he could know that so he could pray with his patients."

"You are in a tizzy today aren't you?" Jan tried to calm her sister down. "Come on, I'll race you to the pier. Let's go for a boat ride. The river always calms me down."

They ran laughing down the steps in the hillside to the platform where their old-timey flat bottomed boat was tied to the pier stretching out over the river a few miles north of Nashville.

"I'll steer, you just rest," Jan said as she eyed her younger sister. She pulled the cord and started the small motor.

"We need to get a bigger motor or a bigger boat," Jeanine muttered as she got in and sat in the seat at the bow of the boat. As she sat down she looked up at the mansion on the opposite cliff above the river and waved at the young man watching them. She felt he was smiling as he waved back.

"Someday I'm going to motor over there and introduce myself to that young man. How long have we been waving at him?" Jeanine laughed. "Here we've lived across the river for years and never have known each other. We've practically grown up together and yet we don't even know who they are."

"Well, we do know something about them," Jan said. "We know there's a father and two sons and a housekeeper, well, at least there are two young men."

"Yeah, it helps to have father's old stargazer out on the promontory where we are queens of all we survey. That young man has grown into quite a looker, wouldn't you say, Jan?" Jeanine loved watching her sister. She was so feminine and her clothes fit so fetchingly. She had the form for it, her thoughts continued ". . . not like me . . . straight as a stick, well, almost."

"Hmm?" Jan acted uninterested and Jeanine knew immediately that she was more interested than she pretended.

When they reached the new Waterfront Park in Nashville, the marvelous new attraction, the paddle wheeler, *The General Jackson* was just leaving its moorings with another group of people aboard. Jan turned off the motor and they rode the waves until there were none left. They both watched as it disappeared and Jan wished out loud, "Some day we're going to take a ride on that boat. I hear the food is delicious and the stage shows are great."

"Maybe we can," Jeanine agreed, "if we sell enough greeting cards." They changed places and Jeanine steered in silence, gazing at the steep cliffs as they passed homes along either side of the river. But her thoughts were busy reminiscing. As long as she could remember they'd lived in the huge, old house that could easily be called a house of seven gables, with its dormer windows and a fireplace in every room. High above the Cumberland, at one time the house had been *the* "house to be invited to" in their neighborhood. They took pride in the fact that their ancestors had walked across the frozen Cumberland to Fort Nashboro with the Robertsons and the Donelsons. With a wrap-around porch their house boasted a parlor where they were only allowed to enter on special holidays when all their family, Mom, Dad, aunts, uncles, cousins and their other sisters Joan and Jennifer were there. They were proud of the wide front hall with the fancy, curved bannister they were forbidden to slide down, but always did, enjoying the sensation of flying through the air and doing something they weren't supposed to do.

Those were the good days, Jeanine thought, happy, carefree days when Mom and Dad and her sisters were still home and life seemed simple. Now Mom and Dad were gone, Joan and Jennifer were married, living in other states and only she, Jan and Aunt Maggie were still at the homestead. Aunt Maggie had come when Jeanine was ten and their mother had died and then just last year their Dad had slipped into eternity with a smile and a "Praise God" on his lips.

Life would be perfect, she thought, if her Dad hadn't wanted a son so much that when she came along, five years after Jan, knowing there would be no more children, he claimed her as his son, named her Billie Jeanine but called her "B.J." and began teaching her all the mechanics he knew about cars. He loved the river, bought a two-man sail boat and taught her everything he knew about sailing and fishing; took her to take tennis lessons until she was better at it than most of the boys she knew. The boys she grew up with were no match for her. They all sized her up as a tomboy, so while her sisters blossomed into real beauties, she was still very much like a boy. She tried to let her hair grow long once, but it was too inconvenient to keep looking pretty and was always in her eyes so she went back to the short haircut she was used to. As soon as she cut it the ends began to curl around her face in a very pixie-like way and she'd kept it that way ever since.

It wasn't until after her father died that Jan, who was the only one left at home by then, and Aunt Maggie, persuaded

4

her to call herself Jeanine, that she began to feel soft and feminine too.

Now as they neared their pier she thought of the two dates she'd had that had turned into near disasters. She'd played tennis with a friend of one of Jan's many boy friends, but she didn't know how to play anything but her best and had beaten him badly. He had never called her agian. The other time was when she'd gone sailing with another young man. They were getting on nicely when he began to swing the boat on its vertical axis to the right when he should have turned the yawl with her head into the wind. Without thinking, Jeanine took over and kept the boat on an even keel, thus losing the friendship of someone she wanted very much to like her.

After that she decided to forget about men, so she read a lot and wrote lots of poems. She had a knack for writing poems for special occasions for friends and family. One day Jan's nimble fingers made a sketch to go with a poem for Aunt Maggie's birthday. She was so pleased, she suggested the girls do more and eventually they had found a market for them in Nashville. It kept them busy and able to afford most of the things they needed or wanted. Whenever they had a batch done, Jeanine used her mechanical skills to get their old Chevy running. Then they'd zip into the big city and make a day of it . . . shopping at one of the malls and eating in a ritzy restaurant. They especially enjoyed going to the restaurant that revolved atop the Hyatt-Regency Hotel. But still she was restless.

As they pulled up to the pier Jan jumped out and tied up the boat, but Jeanine looked at her small sail boat and decided to go out by herself. She'd done it so often no one objected. She loved the busyness of pushing off and the feel when the wind filled the sails and pulled her along so quietly. That's what she liked best. The silence. Just she and the water, the sky and God.

As she sailed past a family in a motor boat she saw a small child leaning over the edge of the boat. She waved to them but her wave turned to fright as she saw the child lose his hold and fall into the river with a splash. She heard the screams. Without another thought she dove in, swam to the child who was coming up for the third time, put her arms around him and swam to where the father circled back and came to a stop near her. She held the child up and loving hands pulled him into the boat, the father scolding and threatening to hide his real fright. Jeanine put her feet on the side of their boat and shoved off to catch her own little sailboat, hearing a "Thank you," floating across the water as she climbed aboard. After that it was time to return home and get into some dry clothes.

As she passed through the living room, she grabbed the newspaper from the sofa. Maybe she would write to that humanist fellow just for fun. He wrote a weekly column called, "Today with Dr. Ben," and the column that made her so angry was on "Depression." His solution was like mind over matter. Think positively. Picture yourself happy and cheerful and pick yourself up by your boot straps and climb right out of those doldrums with a "You can do it" attitude. He may not even get her letter, but at least she'd have the satisfaction of letting him know there was something better.

As she showered and dressed in a cool, yellow linen sun dress with a white peter pan collar, she wondered how she could let him know who Jesus was and what knowing Him could mean for a doctor. Jesus meant so much to her, how could she let him know and not turn him away? One thing was certain, she would write him that night.

Aunt Maggie was her usual cheerful self at dinner, and as always, their meal was punctuated with details of her day. She was a volunteer worker at Vanderbilt Hospital in Nashville and put her whole life into her work. Even though she only went one day a week the patients became her family. She shopped for them and wrote letters for them. Her mind was constantly thinking of them and how she could help them. She seemed a typical, white haired plump grandmother, but both Jan and Jeanine realized she was special and they loved her.

When the kitchen was put in order, Jan had left with her date and Aunt Maggie had retired to her room to write her letters. Jeanine went to her room, to her "office" that she had arranged in one corner of her room with a desk, file cabinet and book shelf.

She picked up the newspaper and turned to the article by Dr. Ben. After reading it her anger was aroused again. Opening a drawer she pulled out a sheet of typing paper, uncovered her typewriter and began typing.

Dear Dr. Ben,

I have read your article on "Depression" in today's paper, and I must say your approach, were I to follow it, would never work. How can a person just say, "I'm not going to be depressed," and just like that the depression will go away? How can you be happy and cheerful unless you have something to be happy and cheerful about, and a person separated from God, can never be completely happy and cheerful unless a person's sins have been forgiven.

I just wanted you to know that Jesus Christ, God's Son, paid the penalty for my sins and now I am not separated from God and I am not depressed, and I am happy and cheerful.

Sincerely yours,

B.J. Pagett

P.S. If you need a Bible for verification, I'll be glad to furnish you one.

Now why did she sign her name like that, she

wondered. Well, why not. Her Dad always called her B.J. and she just added the two "t's" to really disguise herself.

"Oh well," she thought, "he'll never answer, but at least he'll know."

After addressing the envelope to "Today With Dr. Ben" at the newspaper, she slipped into bed and to sleep.

Her dreams were often filled with scenes where she was talking to people about Jesus and they were always shaking their heads and walking away from her. This night her dream was very vivid. She was knocking on a door and the name on it was, "Dr. Ben." In her hand was a Bible. When he opened the door, all she could see was a white coat and head with a mirrored light on it like an eye doctor. He drew her into the room and began looking deep into her violet eyes with his little mirrored light. All the time she was trying to tell him about Jesus and tried to give him the Bible, but he seemed not to hear and only said, "You have beautiful eyes," wrote something on a piece of paper, led her to the door saying, "Come back in two weeks." As the door closed she woke up when she started beating on his door with her fist, calling, "Dr. Ben! Dr. Ben, Jesus is the way out of depression!"

"He must have gotten to me more than I thought," she mused as she slipped out of bed, got a drink of water and returned to her bed, glad that it was just a dream. The rest of her night was dreamless and peaceful.

Chapter 2

Jan and Jeanine drove up their long, straight driveway after picking up their mail from the box out on the road. Looking through the mail Jan picked up a long envelope and held it up to the sun, trying to read through the envelope, laughing at Jeanine.

"Guess what I've got?" she teased.

"A letter. I can see that."

"Yes, but guess who it's from."

"I don't know. Who have you written to?" Jeanine drove the car around to the back of the house.

"Not me, silly. It's for you, from that 'dratted' man you thought would never answer your letter."

"Dr. Ben! I got a letter from Dr. Ben?"

"Yes, my dear sister. I hope you won't be disappointed."

"Why on earth would I be disappointed? I don't even know the man."

Strange that her sister should say that. It's exactly what she was thinking, but why she didn't know.

As soon as the car stopped, she grasped the letter from her sister's hand, ran into the house and up to her room. Breathlessly she plopped herself down in the middle of her single four-poster bed, opened the letter and began to read:

Dear B.J.,
   I am flattered that anyone who feels as you do would bother to read my column at all. I take it you're not

9

exactly a fan.

As to your claims about Jesus Christ, I never gave much credence to that kind of talk. But you wrote so convincingly of your beliefs, I may have to look into it further. I might add that you are like the young Ladybug. You need to come out of your cocoon and see what the world is like.

Thank you for the offer, but believe it or not, I do have a Bible.

Sincerely,
Dr. Ben

A grin spread across Jeanine's face. At least he answered and he didn't tell her to mind her own business, except for that remark about the Ladybug. Did he recognize that she was a female? Or was that just a parallel example he used to tell her she needed to be more earthly minded. Quickly, before she got cold feet, she ran to her desk and typed another letter to Dr. Ben.

Dear Dr. Ben,

I do thank you for taking time to answer my uncomplimentary letter. Please forgive me, but I need to add something to my last letter.

In legal language, a pardon is defined as "a release from the penalty of an offense."

When a governor or other official grants a pardon, he is declaring that the guilty person does not have to undergo the punishment for his crime.

But how much better is God's pardon! The Lord not only declares the sinner free from sin's penalty, He receives him into His family.

I don't understand such love. All I can do is accept it because God said it in John 1:12: "But as many as received him to them gave he power to become the children of God even to them that believe on His name."

By the way, I did agree with your last article and I am

not a Ladybug in the way you mean.

Sincerely,

B.J. Pagett

That should keep him guessing she thought as she sealed and addressed it.

Jan called from downstairs. Jeanine was so happy she fairly flew down the steps. Jan held out a newspaper to her as they went out on the porch to sit in the huge swing that had been hanging there ever since they could remember, still with the same squeak when you reached a certain place in your backward momentum.

"Didn't you tell us you dove off your sail boat to save a little boy who had fallen out of the boat his family was in?"

"Yes. What about it?"

"Look at this letter to the editor." Jeanine read the letter and smiled. It was from the family telling of the incident and since they didn't know who she was they were taking that way of writing their thanks.

"Isn't that nice. I'm glad I could get to him in time."

As they enjoyed the sunset and cool evening breeze of what had been a hot July day, they heard a motor boat which was not unusual. Motor boats went up and down the river all the time, besides barges and most any kind of floating craft. It was a kind of welcome background sound. But this motor sounded much closer and both girls looked down at their pier just in time to see a new motor boat pulling up to it. A young man with blonde, windblown hair jumped up on their pier and then started to climb the steps toward their house. They both got up and started down the hill to meet him. Since they didn't get many visitors from the river, they were anxious to see who he was. As he got nearer both girls eyes met in recognition of the young man who waved to them when they took their boat ride.

"Hi," he grinned breathlessly from the long hike up the

steps. "I'm Tommy Bennett from the house across the river." He pointed to his house. "I thought it was about time we got to know each other after all these years of practically growing up side by side, just one-half mile apart by river."

After welcoming him, they invited him to the porch and Jeanine went in the house returning soon with a tray of iced tea and some of Aunt Maggie's molasses cookies.

"Umm. This is delicious and really hits the spot. So are these cookies." He grinned as he munched. His brown eyes sparkled, lighting up his well-tanned face.

"Well, Tommy, tell us something about yourself," Jan asked.

"Not much to tell. I'm a tennis and golf pro at the Belle Chase Country Club. That's my second home. I'm there most of the time."

"Jeanine's the tennis player in our family," Jan exclaimed.

"Really! Maybe we can play sometime. I can get you in any time."

Remembering her other disastrous date to play tennis, Jeanine was not so quick to take Tommy up on his offer, but then he was a pro so he probably would beat her. She agreed to go with him one day soon but only if Jan went too and he quickly agreed.

"What about the rest of your family?" Jan asked.

"Well, there's just my Dad and Will, my step brother. Will's the smart one in the family. He went to college and works in town. Dad works nights at the newspaper running the printing presses, making sure the paper gets out on time."

He didn't mention that his father's second wife had had money and turned it all over to him, but his pride wouldn't let him live off her money so he worked. She had had the mansion built and they seemed to be a happy family. She'd died many years before.

"We have a housekeeper, Mrs. Phipps. We like to tease her by calling her 'Mrs. Flips.' She acts like she hates it but she really loves it. She's been with us for years and is like a mother to Will and me. Now tell me about you folks."

Jan answered, explaining about Joan and Jennifer and that she and Jeanine and Aunt Maggie were left to keep up the old homestead.

"But don't you have a brother? It seems I've seen a young man around here . . . ." He stopped suddenly and his face got red. "We, a . . . ." He hesitated as Jan and Jeanine started laughing. He looked from one to the other with a puzzled frown on his forehead. They pointed to their father's "stargazer." "We've watched you too. You must have spy glasses."

He laughed easily, relieved, nodding his head. "Yes. But I had a special reason for coming over today. I wanted to congratulate your brother. Where is he?"

"We don't have a brother," Jan's smile was mischievous.

"I guess you mean me," Jeanine said. "I've been Dad's 'son' ever since I was born. What did you want to see 'him' about?" But Tommy was still trying to digest this news.

"You are 'him'?"

Jeanine nodded. "Well," he continued, "I saw what you did on the river the other day and I wanted to congratulate you on your quick thinking. You are an excellent swimmer. You got to that little boy just in time too. I've wanted to come over here ever since to congratulate you. What a brave thing to do."

"It was really nothing." Jeanine felt embarrassed at the attention. She never liked to be the center of conversation.

"Why don't you stay for dinner?" she asked, hoping to get to know him better and to take their minds off her.

"I appreciate the invitation, but I can't tonight. How about a rain check on that. It sounds great."

"Well, we'll be looking forward to that rain check," Jan smiled sweetly at him, then looked away from his penetrating gaze.

Tommy stood up and started down the porch steps, then turned to Jeanine and Jan. "How about some tennis next Tuesday? That's my day off." Looking at Jan he exclaimed, "I wonder why I've waited so long to come over."

"Okay." Jan spoke for the two of them. "What time?"

"How about 10:00 A.M. Bring your swim suits and we'll get a good swim afterward." He ran down the steps, jumped into his boat, waved at them as he lifted the rope off the post and motored back across the river to his own pier.

"Hey, little sister. Things are looking up for us. And isn't he handsome?" Jan was exuberant.

"I said it the other day, sis. He's a looker all right. It should be a fun day."

"But I don't play tennis very well," Jan stated sadly.

"You don't have to, dear. With your long legs and long black page boy no one will care if you hit the ball or not. And while everyone's looking at you, I'll play." Jan hopped up and went into the house, but before Jeanine went in to dinner, she marveled at the beauty of Aunt Maggie's flower garden full of dainty, velvety pansy faces, petunias, cosmos and lavender. She'd even planted monkey grass along the walk around to the back of the house and it's long flowing fingers made a full, graceful border. "God's world," she thought happily, "and I'm part of it."

The next Tuesday Jan answered the phone. It was Tommy. He knew how to cross the river to their home, but he had no idea how to get to their house by road. After talking a few minutes it was decided they would meet him at the county club since it would be too far for him to drive and get there by 10:00. It was strange. He lived so far by land and yet they only lived one-half mile across the river from each other.

He was waiting for them when they arrived at the club and took them in with him. Jan was especially beautiful in her pink and white tennis dress. She'd even tied a pink ribbon around her black tresses to keep them out of her eyes.

Jeanine noticed the look Tommy gave her. Jeanine had stuck to her casual sports costume of khaki shorts and white knit shirt. Not quite beautiful, she just looked petite, clean and fresh with her unmanageable curls and sprinkle of freckles.

On the court she was all business and Tommy soon found he had to be on his toes when he was playing the game with her. She could possibly have been another Chris Everett. But playing Jan was a different story. She certainly was no challenge, but she was no pushover either, when he wasn't noticing how graceful she was.

After an hour's workout they were ready for a cooling swim. Jeanine practiced swimming several laps of the olympic sized pool while Tommy, after some fancy diving, and swimming a couple of laps, swam to the shallower end of the pool where Jan was splashing about.

That morning was the beginning of a beautiful relationship that began with Aunt Maggie, Jeanine and Jan sitting on the porch in the evenings, with Tommy motoring over to visit. It changed about a month later, when Jan took Tommy out to the "stargazer" to look at the stars. Aunt Maggie and Jeanine exchanged looks, then went inside to their rooms.

On one of Tommy's Tuesday's off, Jan and Jeanine went with him on a tour of *The Hermitage,* home of Andrew Jackson. Tommy couldn't believe they had never been to visit a part of U.S. history practically at their back door.

Jeanine loved every minute, going through the famous *Hermitage* mansion with it's six pillared, front veranda, seeing the home of the seventh U.S. president. The front hall was very open, with polished, wide-slatted wooden floors, beautiful hand-painted muraled walls and a lovely curving staircase at the far end. Of course, no one was allowed to enter the rooms but had to look standing behind a velvet cord stretched across the entrances. But to see the huge rooms with horsehair sofas and chairs and extra large hurricane lamps placed on the buffets and in the center of the tables, and try to think of the aristocratic, white haired Andrew Jackson entertaining guests there, was wonderful.

The bedrooms were especially alluring to Jeanine with their mammoth four-poster, canopied beds, so high they had to have stools to stand on to get in and out. She imagined slipping in one of those beds sunk deep in a feather tick mattress with the curtains drawn and piles of feather filled comforts on top. For a moment she wondered who would be sharing the bed with her and then shook those thoughts from her mind, wondering where they had come from.

Out in the back away from the house was the small, one room kitchen and the fireplace with its hooks for pots, a wooden floor with a wooden table in the middle. Andrew Jackson had done a lot of entertaining. How in the world could the cook have prepared such sumptuous meals as curried duck, country hams and other fanciful meals in such a primitive kitchen.

"Lord, thank you for our modern conveniences," she thought as they walked through the unusual square garden, laid out with four paths cutting the square in four parts and meeting in the middle. It was supposed to be an example of early American garden design. Jeanine thought it must be absolutely gorgeous in the spring with tulips, iris, hyacinths and other spring blooming beauties.

Far back of the main house were some log cabins, one of which was said to be the first home of the General and Mrs. Jackson with their very meager and primitive furnishings. She was very glad she had a lovely home and modern bedroom.

As the three of them walked back toward the mansion, Jan and Tommy were immersed in their own personal conversation so Jeanine let them go on ahead. She decided as much as she had enjoyed this tour, she might as well have come alone and from now on she would.

On the way home Jan talked endlessly of Tommy, what he was doing or aspired to do. Jeanine thought, if Jan and Tommy got serious about each other who would do the sketches for her greeting card verses, then thrust the thought from her mind.

As they picked up the mail and drove up the driveway, Jan looked through the letters, junk mail mostly, an endless number of sweepstakes letters, but one letter stood out plainly with a newspaper logo on it. Jan held it up but before she could tease, Jeanine grabbed it and put it in her lap.

"Seems to me you've been getting mail from Dr. Ben for a very long time."

"About six months."

"That's a long time to be writing every week," Jan teased.

"He's become a friend, though I don't think I've changed his mind about Jesus." As Jan raised her eyebrows, she added, "Anyway, he doesn't even know I'm a woman." She opened the car door. Jan slammed her door and hurried around to her.

"Jeanine Page, what do you mean?"

"I've never used Jeanine. I always sign my letters, 'B.J. Pagett,' and don't ask me why I put the two 't's' on our name. I just did."

Jan threw up her arms. "And here all the time I thought you had something going with the good Dr. Ben." Jeanine gave her a weak smiled.

"Don't I wish I did. His letters have really come to mean something to me. It's like I've always wanted, a real meaningful discussion with a man without the man-woman relationship, and yet, I'm finding myself wanting more."

"Well, after this long a time, I'm sure you'd like to meet him in the flesh. I know I would."

"Yes," she said wistfully. "In the meantime I have his letters."

Chapter 3

J eanine rushed to her room to her favorite spot to read "his" letter . . . in the middle of her bed. But today she sat cross-legged, holding his letter to prolong the anticipation. She had a very nice bedroom, she thought. Two windows that opened out over the river with pretty yellow sheers and flowered drapes that picked up the pale yellow in the walls. She even had a fireplace on the opposite side. Sometimes in the winter she'd make a fire in it and curl up in the one flowered and ruffled easy chair to read or to meditate on God's Word. As she looked around, her eyes surveyed the golden oak vanity and chest of drawers with pictures of her Mom and Dad, Joan and Jennifer and their husbands, and took in the nine by twelve braided rug. She'd wanted to be able to see the hardwood floors, even if it meant hard work keeping them clean and shiny, and thought she should be the happiest young woman in the world as she had written Dr. Ben that she was in her first letter. But something was missing. Since Jan and Tommy had become a two-some, it was more evident. Before Tommy, they had done everything together but not anymore and she missed the companionship.

Before she opened her letter she looked at it a long time. Was it possible to love someone who just wrote letters? Someone who didn't even know you were a woman? Someone who didn't even have a face? Most columnists had their pictures above or beside their column, but he didn't. So many times she'd tried to conjure up an image of what she thought he looked like from what his letters told her of his likes and dislikes, and even desires. He would be tall of course, with brown hair with a wave that fell down on his forehead. He'd have clear brown eyes and even if he wore glasses he'd still be handsome. She heaved a big sigh seeing his face in her mind. Most of all, she thought, his smile would go right into her heart. A scripture from Psalm 37:4 came to her mind: "Delight thyself also in the Lord and he shall give thee the desires of thine heart." She closed her eyes. "Lord, I do delight in you. I believe the desire of my heart is to meet Dr. Ben. I think I know him already from his letters. Oh, Lord, give me a chance to tell him about you in person." Then she opened his letter.

> Dear B.J.,
>
> Thank you for your response to the article I wrote last week. Your "insight" into the problem I posed was far more "insightful" than mine and I appreciated your goading me. It is the catalyst I need to make me think more deeply about the Christian principles you're always writing about.
>
> I had to laugh when you said you thought I must be a "dotty old man" trying to think young. I will try to do better.

Jeanine paused and smiled. "I don't really think of you as a 'dotty old man' and I'd be terribly disappointed if you turned out to be," she thought. Then turned back to his letter.

> As always your letters keep me on my toes and make my life one of anticipation for your next missive.
>> I remain your faithful, "dotty old servant,"
>> Dr. Ben

She read the letter again and smiled, thinking, "his letters always make me smile. I wonder if he smiles at mine."

The next Tuesday was Tommy's day off and several weeks before he had suggested they take the three hour sunset dinner cruise on *The General Jackson*. At first Jeanine wanted to decline remembering how alone she felt at *The Hermitage*, but the lure of an evening on a paddle boat was too much, especially since Tommy had made reservations and was going to take them up the river to the boarding platform, dock his boat there near River Front Park and then get it when they returned. The paddle wheeler was to leave the dock at 7:00 P.M. Promptly at 6:15 Tommy's cabin cruiser came humming up to their pier and Jan and Jeanine were waiting, waving to Aunt Maggie watching from the top of their steps.

Jan was a picture of loveliness in tailored mint green slacks, a sheer pale green blouse with one strand of pearls gracing the scoop neckline, with a delicately woven white shawl over her shoulders. Her black hair shone in the fading sunlight and her startlingly blue eyes sparkled brightly under her wispy bangs. As soon as Tommy helped her on board he held her with both hands and pulled her to him for a light feathery kiss.

"Hmm, you look beautiful enough to eat." Then he helped Jeanine into the boat. Jeanine felt underdressed beside Jan and thought angrily that what Jan wore and what she wore had never bothered her before. "Lord are you testing me now because I wrote so positively about my life and feeling to Dr. Ben?" Her navy slacks, white blouse and green bow tie with her navy and green plaid jacket seemed ordinary next to Jan, but she decided this night was an experience she had wanted and nothing was going to stop her enjoyment. The first thing was to enjoy this ride on Tommy's big cruiser.

It was a smooth ride. Tommy knew exactly how to handle the big boat and while Jan stood with him at the wheel, Jeanine sat on the seat behind them, riding backwards, enjoying the sights and sounds of being on the water, watching the houses and sometimes businesses as they passed by. There was a place not far from the park where Tommy "parked" his boat and moored it until they returned. Then they joined the crowds gathering to board *The General Jackson.*

Jeanine went immediately to the deck rail after boarding the sternwheeler to watch the gangplank being raised. A steam calliope began playing somewhere and she began to feel the excitement mounting in her as if she were dressed in crinolines, a belle of the old south. The great paddle wheel began to turn and the magnificent *General Jackson* slowly moved into the current.

Soon they were ushered into a formal dining room where they sated themselves on lobster and shrimp scampi served with sauteed small potatoes, sprinkled with paprika, small sweet peas and onions, a delicious salad and chocolate mousse, all served with tea, coffee or wine. Jeanine wasn't sure Tommy took tea or not because she and Jan had ordered first, but it was a most sumptuous meal.

When the meal was over, the tables were cleared and they were ready for the entertainment of old time songs and dances done in sprightly costumes and talented, professional young performers. Once again Jeanine felt like a belle in crinolines and for a moment would have enjoyed being up on that stage singing those songs and dancing those dances of the gay nineties.

They went up to the top deck to the Victorian Room where there were mirrors everywhere and the lamplight was reflected in the brilliant crystal, brass and authentic gilded ornamentation reminiscent of the days of Mark Twain. There was a grand piano there and a young man who played anything that was requested. She requested "A Bicycle Built for Two," and "Take Me Out to the Ball Game."

Afterward they walked back to watch the paddles churn the water, watching the moonlight jump around in the splashing waves. There were roving performers and costumed entertainers roaming the decks as they enjoyed a soft drink. When the boat pulled up to the dock and let down the gangplank Jeanine didn't want to leave. For a few hours they had been in another world and it had been very pleasant. She thought wistfully, it would have been nice for Dr. Ben to share this experience with her. The ride home on Tommy's boat was full of memories.

She hadn't had a dream for a long time but that night she dreamed she was again knocking on his door with her Bible in her hand. This time he opened the door. His face was just as she had imagined. He took her hand and drew her into the room. "Ladybug, you've come at last and I see you have brought me your Bible. Maybe it will explain things better than mine." Laying it on the table, he took both of her hands and looked into her eyes. "Just as I remembered," he said in a deeply resonant voice. "Your eyes are violet and very beautiful." Then the dream faded away and she slept with a smile on her face.

She made yet one more tour with her sister and Tommy. She hadn't planned to, but she and Jan had been working hard to get a batch of sympathy cards for Mr. Hart, the man whose company was in Nashville. They had even started their own line of cards called "Cherubs." They were small cards, the minimum the post office would allow, with tiny cherubs on the front and cute sayings inside for all occasions. Jan was especially good at drawing the cute eye-catching cherubs in every kind of action. They hoped Mr. Hart would be pleased. Jan deserved this holiday and since Jeanine just imagined Dr. Ben along with her, she didn't mind being a third party. Besides, they always seemed to want her along. Now that she had put a face to her Dr. Ben it wasn't hard. That dream was never far from the back of her mind, especially when he called her, "Ladybug," saying she had beautiful eyes. She'd always thought them as very ordinary, even though they did have a violet tint.

So now they were on their way to Opryland. Tommy was surprised to know they lived so close but had never spent a day there, so he was eager to show them around.

This time they motored over to his pier and climbed the steps to ride with him. They viewed the extraordinary, covered patio. Tommy took them in for a look around before they left. It was like being outdoors, but indoors. A huge paved square with a grass rug, pots of ferns, vining geraniums, bleeding hearts were hanging from the broad cross beams. White rocks lined the outside of the cement floor to the screened room. A huge sun dial stood in one corner and there was rustic, deep cushioned redwood furniture . . . chaise lounge, two wide-armed chairs and round table with redwood benches. A beautiful ceiling fan hung above the table with a center shaded lamp. What a relaxing atmosphere Jeanine thought as she met Jan's shining eyes and sipped some minted tea. Mrs. "Flips" was a sweet faced, round little woman who was pleased as punch that Tommy had brought them in before they left.

Riding in Tommy's fancy Porsche reminded her of the differences in their styles of living, but Tommy had an infectious way about him. He didn't seem to notice the difference and she was happy that he found Jan attractive.

In the parking lot at Opryland Tommy said, "Look for our number on the pole so we can remember where we parked the car. This lot is so huge we could easily get lost. Our pole number is ten." He took each of them by the hand and ran with them to catch the trolley bus that would deposit them at the entrance to the park. There was a window to buy tickets and then several entrance gates. Tommy had bought a map so they could see which way they should go to see the various shows and rides. They had the whole day and by the looks of the schedule Jeanine thought it would take the hole day. They soon found out that standing in line was the most time consuming for any event. It was pleasant walking to the different events for there were flowers everywhere, red and white begonias, geraniums of all colors, and many other green foilage plants in well kept plots. There were cement walls around the flower plots for sitting if you got tired and there was a lot of ground to cover. They planned everything around the main event, "I Hear America Singing," and they didn't mind the wait but they had to get in line early and wait and wait and wait. However, people were friendly and everyone visited with each other and it was soon evident that people were there from many states. The show was well worth the wait and like the stage show on *The General Jackson*, the songs and dances were modern, brilliantly costumed and sung and danced as professionally as any Broadway show. Jeanine wondered how the performers had so much energy. It almost wore her out just listening and watching.

They rode the "Flume," the log that climbed in water, circled around and then flew down the last steep slide and came to a sudden, splashy stop. They were laughing hilariously when they got off, slightly damp. Then there was the old fashioned car ride and the train. They especially enjoyed the "Grizzly River Rampage," where they strapped themselves into a huge, half-barrel contraption. It started on its rolling, turning, dipping ride through smooth water, then rapids and went close to a wall where some unlucky party gets sopping wet by a water fall shooting out from the wall. Jan was the unlucky one who got wet, but Tommy and Jeanine were damp too. They enjoyed that ride so much they got off and went right back for another ride. Jan's slacks were wet but the sun was so hot that by the time they took in a few open air country music shows she was dry and ready for a quick lunch of hot dogs and cokes.

The afternoon drifted away as they lined up and waited or sat in the open air stands and finally Tommy took them to the beautiful Southern Restaurant for some good old southern fried chicken and other delicasies.

It had started to rain while they were in the restaurant so they decided to call it a day. When they came out the rain had let up some, enough so that they decided to make a dash for the entrance to get a trolley bus back to where they'd parked their car. They were not alone in their decision and the only room on the bus was the front seat. It seemed as soon as they got started the rain came down in torrents, slanted right at them. By the time they got off the bus they were already sopping wet and laughing so hard they could barely run. Tommy's and Jan's hair was plastered to their heads. Their clothes were soaked and stuck to their legs while their tennis shoes made squishy noises with every step. Jeanine's hair was a mass of drippy curls. They reached the car and Tommy laughed as he unlocked the doors. "It's a good thing I have leather seats . . . we can't ruin anything."

What a happy day it had been, but Jan and Jeanine were so tired they could hardly wait for their boat to get home. Every so often one of them would break out in a laugh.

"Oh, Jan," Jeanine's laughter floated across the river, "I'll never forget the look on your face when that waterfall fell on you."

Aunt Maggie was waiting for them with towels and mugs of hot chocolate. After that they needed no urging to get to bed.

Chapter 4

Jan and Aunt Maggie had accompanied Jeanine to the airport. She was off to Chicago to be with Joan when she came home from the hospital with her first child. Jan was invited, but she was too interested in Tommy to leave, so Jeanine said she'd go. She had never flown or been to Chicago before and she was only going to be gone two weeks, so it was agreed she would take Jan's place.

It was only an hour's flight to Chicago, but it was Jeanine's first time to fly and she was excited. Kissing them good-bye as her flight was announced, she walked up the boarding ramp right into the plane, handed the stewardess her ticket and was shown to her seat. She had asked for a seat by the window. There was already a handsome young man sitting on the aisle and she had to step over his legs to get to her seat. He was concentrating on papers from his briefcase.

After awhile the "Fasten Seat Belts" light came on and she fastened her belt. She had wanted to be next to a window so she could see the world from high in the sky. The stewardess came to the door of their cabin, picked up a microphone and began giving instructions on where the life jackets were and what to do in case of an emergency.

Jeanine was paying close attention to every word and looking where the stewardess told them to look for their safety items, but the young man seated next to her, although buckled up, was busy with his papers and didn't seem to be paying attention. He must fly a lot Jeanine thought and had heard all this before.

Then the Captain's voice came on the intercom to welcome them aboard Flight #351. "It looks like a beautiful day out there, so sit back and enjoy yourselves."

As they started down the runway Jeanine grabbed hold of the arms of her seat and leaned back, holding on for dear life.

"Your first flight?" the young man asked. She nodded, unable to speak as the plane left the ground and she felt it climbing. What a sensation in the pit of her stomach. Then the plane leveled off for a wide, banking turn and headed north. Finally she dared to look out the window as Nashville became smaller and smaller.

The Captain came on the intercom again and announced: "Please keep your seat belts fastened. We are climbing to 35,000 feet." She felt the plane climbing again and thought to herself, "Lord, keep this plane in the palms of your hands."

At last she relaxed and looked out the window at the marvel of billowing mountains of pure white clouds and here and there the blue, blue sky. "How wonderful!" she thought and sighed.

"It is beautiful, isn't it?" he asked.

"I never dreamed what it would be like up here, but it doesn't seem like this plane is going fast enough to keep us up."

"I know. But I can assure you it is." After a few minutes he asked, "You going to Chicago?"

"Yes, my sister's had a baby and I'm going to help her when she comes home from the hospital."

"What part of Chicago does she live in?"

"The Lincoln-Belmont section I think."

"I know where that is . . . near Wrigley Field."

"I really don't know. I've never been there before." She

turned her head to look out the window. She wasn't used to talking to strangers, even good looking ones with soft, blown dry black hair, dark expressive brown eyes and expensive clothes.

The stewardess came around taking orders for drinks but she shook her head. He asked for some orange juice. He had just finished when he looked at his watch.

"Almost there."

"Already? Seems like we just left Nashville."

"We did . . . and hour ago. Someone meeting you?"

"My sister's husband." Then the seat belt light came on and she buckled her belt feeling the plane start its slow downward descent until suddenly the city was coming up fast and then the plane landed smoothly, rolled down the runway, made a turn, taxied up to it's berth and stopped.

"Well, it was nice sitting with you, little lady. Hope your stay in Chicago is a happy one."

"Thank you. I enjoyed the flight." Then everyone was scrambling to get off. She went down the ramp into the waiting room and looked around.

"Jeanine, over here!" Jim called and she hurried over to her brother-in-law, gave him a hug and kiss. They left to go get her bag from the rolling baggage belt. As they were waiting, her seat mate walked her way but did not stand by her but rather he greeted Jim with a slap on the back.

"Jim! Long time, no see. How're things in the insurance business?"

"Bob . . . doing okay, and the brokerage business is doing well I see." Jim looked Bob over, then turned to Jeanine. "This is my sister-in-law, Jeanine Page."

"Well, it was nice sitting next to you on the plane, Miss Page, but even better knowing your name." Her brother-in-law then introduced her to the young man.

"Jeanine, this is an acquaintance of mine, Bob Stillman." Jeanine acknowledged the introduction with a slight dip of her curly head. Her bag came by and Jim picked it off the belt. They turned to leave when Bob called, "Nice to meet you, Miss Page."

"Yes, thank you," Jeanine spoke shyly. Jim took her arm and led her to the huge parking garage to get his car. It took them forty-five minutes to get to their apartment in one of those many look-alike brownstone, two flat houses. Their apartment was on the second floor.

He had brought Joan home from the hospital that day. She was waiting for them, sitting in an easy chair in her quilted robe, holding little "Jim, Jr."

"Jeanine . . . I'm so glad you could come. Look at our precious."

Jeanine leaned over the baby and kissed her sister, admiring the tiny boy in her arms. Even at the tender age of four days, he already looked like Jim. He had his forehead and eyes.

"How are you feeling?" Jeanine asked.

"Not too spry right now, but I got along fine, so I should be plenty strong by the time you leave."

"Well, I guess you're ready for some dinner. I'll just take off my things and get out in the kitchen and fix us something simple for tonight."

"Soup will be fine, and a salad," Joan suggested. "There's some vegetable soup in the refrigerator I fixed. It should still be good."

While Jim and Joan talked and gazed at their new son, Jeanine busied herself in the kitchen and soon had a green salad ready, hot soup and rye bread with cheese wedges.

Joan was strong enough to come to the big, round table in the kitchen, so while the baby slept they had a chance to visit as they ate. Joan was radiant. Jeanine thought she looked like Jan.

Joan wanted to know what was happening in Nashville, so Jeanine filled her in on Tommy and Jan's romance, their trip to the *Hermitage, The General Jackson*, their day at Opryland, about their new line of greeting cards called "Cherubs," and dear Aunt Maggie.

"Well, I hope you and Jan have a lot of success. It sounds like they should be popular." After visiting awhile longer Joan went to her room, Jim read the newspaper and Jeanine, after cleaning up the kitchen, was ready for bed. Since Joan was nursing the baby she wouldn't be needed during the night.

Before she went to sleep, Jeanine thought of Dr. Ben and hoped Jan would forward any letters from him. She hadn't mentioned him to Joan and wouldn't unless she got a letter.

The next day was pure joy in bathing the baby with baby oil. She learned you don't use water the first few days. When he was clean and powdered, with a fresh gown, he smelled just like a baby ought to smell. She kissed the soft, smooth sweet smelling skin at the nape of his neck. He only cried when he was hungry and Joan was ready and eager to feed him and cuddle him closely.

When the baby was asleep, Jeanine washed all his baby things from the day before and even let her imagination run its gamut thinking of herself and a baby boy who looked like Dr. Ben. She smiled at herself as she folded soft, fluffy receiving blankets, tiny baby shirts and gowns.

While Joan and the baby napped, she wrote verses for the "Cherubs" line. She even took a short nap herself before it was time for lunch.

Joan and Jim had a tiny square of a back yard where she could walk. They were only a block and a half away from the ball park that the young man on the plane had mentioned, so she took walks down there and back.

There were diapers to change but for the most part she didn't have much to do. Joan slept most of the time for two days, then began to spend more time with Jeanine.

One evening around 5:00 P.M. the phone rang. Jim

31

wasn't home yet and Joan was lying down, so Jeanine answered it.

"Henderson's residence," she said.

"Well, Hello, Jeanine is it?"

"Yes?" She wondered who could possibly be calling her in Chicago.

"Remember me . . . your seat mate on Flight #351?"

"Oh, yes, Mr. Stillman. Did you want to speak to Jim?"

"No. I prefer talking to you. I don't believe Jim would fit into my plans."

"What do you mean?"

"I mean, I would like to get better acquainted with you. I was wondering if I could take you out to dinner and perhaps take in something cultural, or whatever you'd like to do."

"Well, I'd have to think about it. I don't even know you."

"That's my point. I want to know you and I hope you'd like to know me." For a minute his handsome face flashed before her eyes.

"Well, I certainly appreciate your thoughtfulness, but I couldn't possibly go with you tonight."

"When, then?" What was it about him that made her wary?

"I'll have to think about it."

"Okay, Miss Page. I'll call you in a couple of days. In the meantime think about it."

Jeanine hung up the phone as Jim walked in.

"Guess who just called me?" she said.

"I'm no good at guessing games," Jim smiled. "Who?"

"Bob Stillman."

"What did he want?"

"To take me out."

"You going?"

"I told him I wouldn't go tonight, but he's going to call back in a couple of days. What do you think of him?"

"He's a nice enough chap, I guess. I only know him

through business circles. I haven't heard anything against him. Why don't you go. It will be a chance to see something of Chicago since I will not be able to show you around. It will be a nice change for you. You might even like him."

When Bob called two days later, Jeanine decided to have dinner with him, gave him Joan's address and was ready for him when he rang the bell. Jim ran down the steps and opened the door, brought him up to their apartment for a few minutes. Jeanine had been unable to do anything with her unruly black curls, but had chosen a dressy black suit with a sheer white blouse. A gold chain with a single tear drop pearl on it hung around her neck and a gold heart stick pin was in her jacket lapel.

When Bob Stillman saw her he whistled and smiled engagingly. "I don't even need to go to dinner. You look good enough to eat." Jeanine blushed as she often did when she was the center of attention. She picked up her gloves and purse, and her beige coat with the brown fur collar. Bob jumped to hold it and helped her into it. Jeanine was quick to move away in case he had inclinations of lingering with his hands on her arms.

They said their goodbyes and Jim went down stairs to let them out.

"Just ring the bell when when you get back. I'll come down and let you in," he instructed Jeanine and wished them a happy evening.

Bob put his hand under her elbow and held it there until they got to his white Lincoln. She wasn't so sure she'd done the right thing, accepting his invitation when she didn't even know him . . . but that's why they were going out. He'd said, ". . . to get acquainted."

He took her to a very elegant restaurant called *The King's Court*, off Michigan Avenue somewhere. In the car she sat near the door. Bob laughed, "You don't need to be afraid of me, Jeanine. I won't bite." She laughed in spite of herself. He parked the car and opened her door, then held her elbow on the way into the restaurant. He had called ahead and made reservations. They stood and waited until a waiter in a tuxedo came up to Bob. "Mr. Stillman? Right this way please." He escorted them to a table with a linen table cloth and napkins folded and standing on their edges before each place. The waiter bowed. "My name is Walter, and I will be your waiter for the evening." He gave them each a menu and said politely, "I'll be back to get your order when you have had a chance to choose." He bowed again and left.

What fancy looking menus, large and shiny with the name of the restaurant engraved on the front. When Jeanine saw the prices she wondered, but decided if Bob couldn't afford this place he wouldn't have brought her here, so she ordered a Filet of Beef served with Bernaise sauce, rice pilaf, a green salad, French bread and tea. For dessert she decided on cold lemon souffle with raspberry sauce. She noticed Bob ordered the Prime Rib of Beef.

When their food was served, she lowered her head for a brief blessing and raised her eyes to see a question in Bob's eyes, but felt no need to explain. She felt shy at first, but as the meal progressed, Bob was quite charming and made her talk about the things nearest her heart, except Dr. Ben, of course. It really was very enjoyable and when they were through he asked her what she wanted to do.

"I think I'd like to walk on Michigan Avenue and look in the windows. I've heard a lot about it."

"That's fine with me." So they walked and talked and the windy breezes blew through her curls. She found it quite invigorating. They window shopped and talked about their likes and dislikes in the clothes they saw. He never even tried to hold her hand for which she was grateful, but of course he couldn't because she kept her hands in her pockets to keep them warm.

"Next time I walk on Michigan Avenue, I'll wear a scarf,"

she exclaimed laughing, her cheeks rosy from the breeze.

"I'm glad you said that, Jeanine. I want there to be a next time. In fact, I was thinking of next Saturday. I'd like to take you to the Dunes National Park. Have you ever been there? It's only a thirty mile drive."

"No. This is my first visit to Chicago."

"Well, actually, it's in Indiana, but not too far away from the Chicago area. Will you go with me? I'll bring a picnic."

"A picnic? In January?"

"We'll make it a first."

"Well, I'll have to see what Joan's plans are. After all, I came up here to take care of her and the baby."

"Okay then, I'll call you on Friday."

She had begun to shiver from the wind and he suggested, "We'd better get back to the car before I have an ice baby on my hands." He laughed and she tried to laugh but her teeth were chattering.

"Come on," he challenged. "The best thing for that is running." So they started to run back to where he'd parked the car. She was lagging behind so he reached for her hand and she did pull it out of her pocket and he pulled her with him to his car.

They were breathless when they got there. He unlocked the door and helped her in, then got a lap robe from the back seat and put it over her lap.

"Thank you. That feels great," she said with teeth that were still chattering.

He got in and turned the key. The engine purred and it wasn't long until warm air began to send its welcome heat to her.

"I hope you won't catch a cold from this, but I loved every minute."

"It was fun." She was surprised at herself. He really was very nice.

At the house, he walked with her to the door, but he

never touched her. When she'd rung the bell, he just said, "Thanks for coming tonight. I'll call you."

"Thank you, Bob. I enjoyed it." Jim let her in and saw her rosy cheeks.

"How'd it go?"

"It was a very nice evening. He wants to take me to the Dunes National Park next Saturday.

"He try anything?"

"No. He was a gentleman in every way."

"That's good. I was a little worried."

"Does Joan need me for anything before I go to bed?" she asked.

"No. Everything's fine."

"Then I'll go to bed. Thanks for waiting up." Jeanine went to sleep reliving the evening. "Yes," she thought, "Bob Stillman is a very charming fellow."

Joan was up more every day and took over bathing and dressing little "Jimbo," so Jeanine's duties were mainly washing the baby's things every day, cooking meals and keeping the house clean. She looked every day for a letter from Dr. Ben, but it never came.

She had time for walks, reading and writing her greeting card verses. There would be plenty for Jan to illustrate when she returned home. There was lots of time for reading and *Wuthering Heights* was a thick book, which she was enjoying very much.

When Bob called, she'd decided to go with him since they would be coming back that same night.

He picked her up at 8:00 A.M. Saturday morning. It took longer to get through the Chicago traffic than it did to get to the Park once they got out of the city. The Park was just a nice drive away and Bob seemed to know how to bring her out of her shyness. The white Lincoln was a dream to ride in. As they drove they talked about a lot of things. But later, she thought, he never talked much about himself at all.

The Dunes was a startling place to see. Acres and acres of nothing but rolling hills of sand. She was glad she had dressed in warm sport togs for this outing. She was wearing a grey jogging outfit trimmed in wine. It even had her name embroidered in wine on the zip-up jacket. She was glad she'd thought to bring along her all-weather hooded shortie coat as the wind along the lake was quite chilling on this January day, even though the sun was shining. Her jogging shoes were just right for the deep rolling hills and hills of sand, as far as they could see, all the way down to the beach near the lake. It had not snowed for a week so there were no skiers but still there were plenty of people who had braved the winds to come out and hike on one of the many tails. The rangers were there to guide when needed.

Hiking was slow but fun as they found shells of different kinds and sometimes unusual looking pieces of weathered wood. When she found one small enough, Jeanine put it in her pocket for a souvenir. Bob found her a nautilus shell which she thought was quite intriguing.

He held her hand as they walked. Sometimes down close to the shore where they could run, they jogged some or chased each other, laughing and breathless from the wind. When she started to shiver he suggested, "It's time for some hot coffee and lunch I think." He led her to one of the many shelters scattered here and there, where he had put the picnic basket, took out a large thermos and poured coffee into the mug she held with mittened hands. It was delicious and just what she needed.

Her hood had fallen down and her curls were blowing every which way. She knew her cheeks must be rosy red from the wind. Bob's soft, brown eyes got deeper when he looked at her. When she saw that look, she wished Jim was there.

However, Bob found a bench and table, had her sit on the lap robe and brought it across her lap to take the chill from her legs. His hands lingered a moment longer than she felt was necessary on her legs. She laughed to hide her embarrassment.

"We must be crazy to have a picnic out here in January, but I'm so glad I got to see the Dunes. I wouldn't have believed it if I'd been told what they were like."

Bob handed her a chicken salad sandwich and some potato chips on a paper plate. She had to use one hand to keep the plate from blowing away and they laughed together trying to hold everything down.

"Jeanine, I wouldn't have missed this day for anything. Even though it is a crazy day for a picnic, I hope you're enjoying it as much as I am." His eyes were warm as they held hers.

He certainly was nattily dressed in the latest sports outfit money could buy, in navy and tan. He was about the handsomest man she'd ever known.

"Thank you for asking me." Jeanine looked away from his eyes. Maybe she was reading too much in them, but it was far too soon.

When they finished their lunch they took one more walk along the beach. The water looked dark and cold and suddenly, to Jeanine it looked foreboding. She turned to Bob.

"Would you mind if we went home now?"

"Why? Have I done something wrong?"

"Not yet," she thought, but said, "Not at all. I'm just very cold and feel I should go home and get warm." Without another word he agreed. They gathered up the lap robe and picnic basket. He took her hand and led her to the car. Once inside she leaned her head back on the seat and closed her eyes.

"Being out in the cold weather makes me sleepy, and your plush car is so comfortable and warm."

"Jeanine, I don't want this day to end," he said. "There's a neat little cafe just inside Chicago where we could stop and get some coffee, or cocoa if you prefer, and a sweet roll." But his words dwindled away as she fell asleep, her head turned toward him on the plush upholstery of the seat.

She woke up when Bob stopped the car at her sister's apartment building. He leaned over and kissed her on the forehead.

"Bob, what are you doing?"

"You looked so much like a pixie I couldn't resist." He had his hand on the seat above her head and was smiling at her in his charming way, but Jeanine was still groggy and not ready for his kiss.

"When can I see you again?" he asked.

"Bob, I'm going home in another week. I don't think it's right for me to take up your time like this."

"Jeanine!" he exclaimed. "Do you think I'm just taking up time with you? I enjoy being with you and I want to see you as much as possible before you go back to Nashville. I'd like to see you Monday, Tuesday, Wednesday, Thursday . . . every night until you leave."

"That's quite impossible," Jeanine stated. "I'm here to take care of Joan and the baby and I feel I'd be neglecting my duty if I went out every night. However, I will agree on one more evening. There's a special showing of Renoir's paintings at the Plummett Art Gallery on Tuesday evening. I'd like to go to that if you'd like to take me. It begins at 7:00 o'clock. Are you interested?"

"To be with you, yes. To see art painting, even Renoir's, not too much. But I'm willing to go in order to be with you. I'll be by about 6:30 if that's all right with you."

He walked her to the door and before she knew what was happening, he'd pulled her to him and brushed her lips with his . . . nothing passionate, just a touch.

"I like you a lot, Jeanine Page. See you Tuesday." Then he left her to ring the bell for Jim and by the time Jim opened the door she was watching the retreating red lights on his car, wondering about what had just happened.

As Joan was now so much stronger, Jeanine and Jim felt free to leave her on Sunday morning to go to their church. She joined her sweet soprano to Jim's deep rumble as they rejoiced in the Lord together in singing the songs she loved . . . "What a Friend We Have in Jesus," and "Sweet Hour of Prayer."

Sunday afternoon everyone was lazy so while the rest of the family napped, she continued reading Emily Bronte's *Wuthering Heights*. She read until her eyes go heavy and she fell asleep in her chair.

All day Monday and Tuesday, Jeanine wondered about going out with Bob again. By dinner time she had almost talked herself out of going. Maybe Bob would just come in and spend a pleasant evening with them. She could pop some corn and there were soft drinks in the refrigerator. She told Jim when Bob came to bring him up. She'd talk to him about staying. However, she had dressed in her black suit and white blouse, so when Bob came up, he would not hear of staying home, saying Jeanine had asked to see the paintings and he was keeping his promise to take her. Reluctantly, she went with him, promising herself they'd stay at the gallery as long as possible. She didn't even know why. So far he'd been a real gentleman.

The gallery was much larger than she'd ever imagined. Being a special showing there were many people. Elegantly furnished with velvet draperies, fashionable furniture and viewing rooms where people could be shown a picture they might be interested in buying, she enjoyed looking around. Going from room to room she stopped in front of every picture, whether she understood what it was trying to portray or not. She did not want to be alone with Bob. She wondered why she'd even made this date.

Reading whatever there was to be read about each painting, she could feel Bob's eyes on her. Even though there were lots of people milling about, they all talked in muted voices and it seemed almost like a library. Once Bob started to speak to her and he sounded so loud she put her fingers to her lips, then saw the look of frustration on his face. How long could she keep him like this? Once when a hostess asked if they were looking for anything in particular, she shook her head.

After an hour and a half, she decided she couldn't keep him there any longer. He'd been very patient.

"Okay," she turned to him, "let's go. I've seen all I need to see." With a sigh of relief he helped her on with her coat and outside helped her to his car.

"There's a coffee shop around the corner. We can go there and talk."

They entered the room with it's steamed up windows and found it a very bright, homey place with cozy tables and a kind of tea room atmosphere. He chose a table back in a corner.

"This okay?" he asked.

"Fine with me." She would try to be friendly, since, after tonight she'd not see him anymore.

After the waitress took their orders Bob turned his soft, brown eyes on her.

"So, you're going back to Nashville? And who have you got there that makes you so anxious to get back?"

"No one. I have my greeting card business. My sister and I have started a new line of small greeting cards called 'Cherubs.' We're having quite a demand for them and we're quite excited about it."

"I can believe it. Your eyes are sparkling. Jeanine, you really are quite lovely." She laughed.

"Thank you, but I have a mirror. You should see my sister, Jan. She's beautiful, like Joan and Jennifer, my other sisters." Her small hands lay resting on the table by her dessert plate, toying with the utensils and glass of water.

Bob put his hands over them and immediately she tensed up inside. What was the matter with her? Any girl would feel in heaven dating this handsome man.

"Jeanine, I don't suppose I could persuade you to stay longer?"

"I'm afraid not. Joan is strong enough now. I could leave anytime, but my return ticket is for next Sunday."

They had finished their chocolate eclairs and coffee. She picked up her gloves.

"Must we leave?"

"Yes. I need to get home."

"Do you ever do anything crazy . . . like breaking Jim's curfew? Or are you always the dutiful little sister?"

"Whatever for would I want to stay out 'after Jim's curfew,' as you call it?" she asked innocently.

"I could think of a lot of reasons," he answered with a wink. Jeanine couldn't wait to get home. Bob was out of her league and she felt he expected something of her she wasn't willing even to think about.

When they got to the apartment, he left the car running so there would be heat, but he made no move to get out of the car. Jeanine reached to open her door. Her move was futile as he grasped her arms and pulled her to him, enfolding her in his arms.

"Jeanine, I think you need to be kissed as you've never been kissed before." His lips pressed down on hers in a buising, crushing kiss. She tried to pull away, but he had her arms pinioned under his and she could not move.

"Please, Bob. I don't understand why you're doing this."

"Oh, I think you do. You've been playing 'come on' with me every time we've been together and I think I've been patient long enough." She tried to deny it, but knew it was useless now.

With a silent prayer to the Lord for help, she pushed with all her strength, grasped the door handle, opened it and practically fell to her knees trying to get out. She ran to the door and started to ring the bell, but Jim opened it before she could push it. Why had she not seen the subtle hints along the way?

"I've been watching from the window and decided you'd been down here too long, so I came down to see what was wrong." As he closed the door they heard the squeal of tires as the big, white Lincoln sped down the street.

"Oh, Jim," she sobbed as he put his arms around her. "I've been such a fool. He wanted me to . . ." She sobbed and sobbed. Why, oh why, did all her dates turn out wrong? She'd just stick to writing letters. That was much safer and so was Dr. Ben. Now she couldn't wait to get home. Surely there would be letters from him waiting.

And there were. Two wonderful letters that made her heart rejoice again.

Chapter 5

Jeanine was so excited she could hardly contain herself as she flew down the stairs to breakfast. Today she and Jan were going to see Mr. Hart and would learn how he liked their "Cherubs" selections. Jan was already seated and Aunt Maggie, after the blessing, quickly set her orange juice before her, then proceeded to serve her scrambled eggs, done with cheese and a bit of onion as she liked them, a couple of strips of crisp bacon and a hot mug of black coffee. She buttered herself a piece of nicely browned toast.

"You girls better eat up and get going. We don't want you to keep that nice Mr. Hart waiting."

Jeanine and Jan smiled at each other. Aunt Maggie still treated them as she did when they were teenagers. This was Friday and Aunt Maggie's day to go to Vanderbilt Hospital, so they would drop her off on their way. Mr. Hart's office was not too far from Vanderbilt.

After seeing him they planned to go way out the super highway to a new mall called, Hickory Hollow, just to look around.

Aunt Maggie talked all the way into Nashville. "I do hope Mrs. Fuller is feeling better today. She was so nauseated after her operation. I think it must have been her medicine. And then there's that lady in room #519. I can't remember her name, but she liked having me read to her."

When they dropped her off Jan smiled. "Bless her heart.

She does so much good for those patients. I know they're glad to see her come."

"I'm sure the nurses are too," Jeanine added. "Some of those patients can be cantankerous but Aunt Maggie takes it right out of them."

Jeanine found a parking spot, put some money in the meter and they went in to Mr. Hart's office. He greeted them with a smile that lit up his round face and balding head.

"Come in girls. I have good news for you. I showed your "Cherubs" cards to a prospective buyer from a Christian bookstore and he liked them so much he wants exclusive rights to them. It will mean more money for you. You really deserve more than we can pay, so I'm really happy for you. 'Bring me all you can.' That's what the man said." He gave them a check for their last batch and they left his office in high spirits, made their way to the bank to make their deposit, then headed out toward the super highway and Hickory Hollow Mall.

It was beautiful with all their favorite stores, Sears, Penneys, Lerners and one new store they had never heard of before, Botony and Lowes, for more expensive tastes. But it was fun to browse. There were beautiful trees growing in the mall in huge round pots with open sky lights that gave the trees room to grow beyond the ceiling. There was also a pool where people dropped money and a special place to eat that was a large square, dropped about three feet with steps, tables and chairs, surrounded by every kind of quick food place imaginable. They decided to try the Chinese cuisine and ordered Chicken-on-a-stick with a rice dish with all kinds of vegetables and bits of scrambled egg and of course, egg rolls and Fortune cookies. They opened their cookies first. Jan's said, "You have long life kiddo." They were still laughing as Jeanine opened hers which said, "Happiness to come your way soon."

"Maybe that means you'll meet Dr. Ben," Jan said.

"I think that would be happiness . . . but maybe it wouldn't. I think maybe I should stop writing to him."

"Why? You love his letters," Jan exclaimed.

"I know. I love them too much. I imagine all kinds of things about him and I even dreamed about him the other night. He's got a face now and that's wrong. He's a doctor and probably married with umpteen children."

"You don't know that," Jan chided.

"I don't know otherwise either."

"But do you think if he were happily married and a family man, he'd be writing you all these letters?"

"Maybe not . . . oh!" Jeanine grabbed the side of her neck.

"What's the matter?" Jan asked with a worried frown.

"I had a sharp pain that shot up the side of my neck. But it's gone now." They finished their meal, talking about their new "Cherubs" line of cards and each was like a catalyst to the other. Jeanine telling her ideas for poems and Jan giving her ideas of illustrating them.

"We'll have to start on them right away," Jan said, then looked at Jeanine in alarm as she grasped the side of her neck again.

"Did you have another pain?"

Jeanine nodded. "I must have caught a cold in my glands. Maybe we should stop and see Dr. Hamilton on our way home. He'll probably have something to give me for it. This January weather is so uncertain." She explained the pains away.

They went by the hospital and picked up Aunt Maggie and told her they needed to stop by Dr. Hamilton's office for some cold medicine.

Aunt Maggie and Jan went in with her. Dr. Hamilton had been their family doctor for many years and it was always good to talk to him. At that time of day he was winding down on patients so they didn't have to wait long.

Jeanine told the kindly grey haired doctor about the two shooting pains in her neck. He examined her neck and lymph glands under her chin. Then he donned a pair of rubber gloves and examined her mouth, feeling all around her tongue. He took off his gloves and told her to wait a moment. Then he disappeared into another office and she heard him talking in a low voice to someone on the phone. When he came back he was not smiling.

"Jeanine, you don't have a cold. I don't know what you've got, but I've made an appointment for you for tomorrow morning to see a friend of mine, Dr. Goldstein. He's an Eye, Ear, Nose and Throat specialist and he can tell you more than I can. Your appointment is at ten o'clock at the Medical Arts Building near Vanderbilt." He gave her a little card with Dr. Goldstein's name and the time of her appointment on it.

They drove home in silence, each wondering what could possibly be wrong.

As she lay in bed, Jeanine talked to the Lord as she often did. "Dear Lord, you know everything there is to know about me and you know what's wrong with me that I should have to see this doctor. My life is in Your hands, do with me what you will." Having turned her body over to the Lord she went soundly to sleep.

The next day, Jan and Aunt Maggie accompanied her to Dr. Goldstein's office. They stayed in the waiting room while Jeanine went into the inner sanctum of this doctor's suite of rooms.

First of all there were x-rays from all angles of her throat and neck and then there was the wait while the x-rays were being developed. At last Dr. Goldstein called her into his office.

"Do you mind if my sister and my Aunt come in with me? I'm not married and I want them to hear what you have to say."

"Of course not. Bring them in." He had a kindly face and demeanor. When they were all seated, Dr. Goldstein's compassionate eyes and wavy hair stayed in Jeanine's mind like a photograph, never to be forgotten, as he looked at them. He held up the x-rays to explain what he was going to say.

"Miss Page, you have a tumor on your salivary gland. Are you sure the pains you experienced are the first you've had? It's quite a large tumor."

"I've not had any before." Jeanine's heart was pounding.

"I must make a biopsy of course. It may be benign, but it could be malignant . . . but let's not cross that bridge until we come to it, shall we?" he smiled. "I'd like to have you in my office at 8:30 Monday morning. We'll know more after that."

They left his office in silence until they got to the car.

"It's probably benign," Jan said as they rode home.

"I know it's cancer," Jeanine said in a matter of fact voice. They looked at her stunned.

"You don't know that until after the biopsy," Aunt Maggie scolded.

"Don't you see?" Jeanine's eyes were sparkling. "I asked God to help me win Dr. Ben to Him. God is letting me have this cancer and will help me to get well so I can be a better witness to Dr. Ben. How can Dr. Ben refuse to believe in Him when I am well?"

"Jeanine, you are not facing reality," Jan exclaimed exasperatedly, with a worried frown on her forehead.

"I know my Lord won't let me down. Cancer is nothing to Him."

Her mind was fixed and nothing Aunt Maggie or Jan said could dissuade her from her line of thinking, so they gave up and simply made this a matter of private prayer.

Monday morning Jan drove and Aunt Maggie accompanied Jeanine to Dr. Goldstein's office. Jeanine appeared to be perfectly calm, but Jan and Aunt Maggie's hearts were full of pain.

Dr. Goldstein showed Jeanine to a room with an examining table and told her to lay on the table with her head near the end where there was a sink on the wall.

"I'm going to have to take a piece out of the bottom of your tongue. You understand?" Jeanine smiled and nodded. She'd asked the Lord for a verse of scripture to give the good doctor, so while he was washing his hands she asked, "Do you know Isaiah 26:3?"

"No," he answered. "What is it?"

"It says, 'Thou wilt keep him in perfect peace whose mind is stayed on thee because he trusteth in thee.' I'm trusting in the Lord," she said.

"Well, that's fine," Dr. Goldstein said. Just then another doctor came in the room, evidently to assist Dr. Goldstein, but he said, "I won't need you. I've never had a patient like this." The other doctor left and Dr. Goldstein proceeded to take the piece from her tongue.

Then he told her to come back Thursday afternoon for the results. Her tongue was still rather numb and seemed to be swelling so her talking was slurred. She said something about only wanting a milk shake that night so they stopped on the way home to get her the chocolate shake.

The next few days she and Jan were busy on their new line of cards. Her tongue was still swollen so she couldn't eat anything but wanted only shakes or something she could drink. For Jan and Aunt Maggie the days dragged, but Jeanine was peaceful, and didn't seem to be worried or afraid. Jan and Aunt Maggie were very frightened. To them cancer was a scary word.

Thursday dawned bright and crisp. A sunny January day. It should have been a happy day. Jan and Jeanine had done enough "Cherub" designs for their first consignment. They were quite happy with the way the cards had turned out. Jeanine envied Jan's way with her feather-lite brush drawings.

She felt they were what sold her little ditties.

All the time she was getting ready to go see Dr. Goldstein for the results of the biopsy, she was singing a chorus they sang at church:

"My wonderful, wonderful Saviour,
My wonderful, wonderful Lord.
He lights up my days
With happy thoughts
And all my nights with praise."

She knew in her heart the doctor would tell her she had cancer but she believed He could take care of something like her turmor so there was nothing to fear.

At Dr. Goldstein's office, he seated them all and after some small talk he said seriously, "Well, I wish I had some good news to tell you, but I don't. You have a malignant tumor on your salivary gland and the sooner it comes out the better."

Jan and Aunt Maggie gasped and tears popped into their eyes, but Jeanine was as calm as if he had told her he thought it would snow soon.

Dr. Goldstein picked up a skull and with his pencil showed them what he planned to do. He drew a line from one ear to the other. "There will have to be a cut from ear to ear, another cut through your lip and down through your neck to meet the other cut. I will have to take everything out under your tongue, quite a bit of your tongue, all your lower gums and part of your chin bone and most of your lower teeth. I'll leave one tooth on one side, the last one, and the last two on the other side. Hopefully, a dentist can make you some teeth and hook them on to the teeth that are left."

He looked at them all for a moment to let all that sink in.

"Do you have any questions?"

"I understand," Jeanine said steadily. Jan and Aunt Maggie were speechless at the enormity of what he planned to do to their precious loved one.

"Then I want you at Vanderbilt Hospital Saturday afternoon about 2:00 P.M. Monday morning Dr. Cardwell will put radium needles through your tongue into the tumor. This will help to shrink the perifery. He'll take them out on Thursday and hopefully, I should be able to operate on Friday. I'll be at the hospital to check you in."

"Thank you, Dr. Goldstein. I think we need to go home and pray," Jeanine said evenly without a trace of fright.

"Fine. That's what you should do," he replied and went to the door with them.

When they got to the car, Jan's eyes were full of tears. She blew her nose a couple of times.

"I don't see how you can stay so calm after what he said."

"I told you, Jan, God has a reason for this. I believe it is for Dr. Ben, so why should I be afraid?"

"But Dr. Ben won't even know."

"He will when it's over. I plan to go to the newspaper and meet him."

"He's not at the newspaper. He probably just drops his article off each week and leaves." Jan was feeling frustrated.

"Well, I'll just have to call and find out where he lives, won't I?"

Her tongue was still a little swollen so it was hard to talk. Jan realized how futile it was to argue with Jeanine in this mood. All she could do was pray and hope Jeanine was right, but what grabbed at her heart was that Jeanine may be placing her trust too strongly and she could die. A quick sob escaped but she held it in check. She must be brave for Jeanine's sake.

They picked up the mail on their way and there was a letter from Dr. Ben. Jeanine had stopped writing him for over a month now. She wondered what he could be writing about.

Since she was still drinking milk shakes, she took it and went to her room. As usual, she sat in the middle of her bed and opened the letter.

My Dear B.J.,

For months now you have faithfully written me letters that have thoroughly entranced me with your wit and insight, so why you have stopped writing me now I do not know.

I hope I have not written something that has turned you completely against me

Please tell me what I have done to cause you to stop writing. Take up your pen again. I would hate to think you had laid it down forever. You have much more talent in that pen than you know.

Your grateful servant.
Dr. Ben

Jeanine read the letter sadly for the second time. She'd missed his letters more than she cared to admit. She must stick to her resolve not to write any more because she felt she was falling in love with the writer and she didn't even know him.

"When all this is over, Dr. Ben, you'll know. You'll know."

Chapter 6

On Friday night, Tommy motored across the river to be with Jan, Aunt Maggie and Jeanine on this night before she went into the hospital. There were telephone calls of love and encouragement from Joan and Jennifer. Then they sang hymns and each one prayed, even Tommy, in a halting, sincere way. There were some tears in Jan and Aunt Maggie's eyes and even Tommy wiped his eyes. But Jeanine was as cheerful as ever, convinced God was allowing her to have this cancer to prove to Dr. Ben that He could take care of it.

That night before she went to sleep she repeated all of the scriptures she knew to give her peace. The last ones were Philippians 4:6, 7: "Be anxious for nothing but in everything by prayer and supplication let your requests be made known unto God. And the peace of God which passeth all understanding, shall keep your hearts and minds through Christ Jesus." Then she prayed softly, "Thank you Lord, for what you are going to do through this operation." Then she went to sleep without even a dream.

Saturday afteroon, Tommy came over and went with them to the hospital. They sat in the waiting room downstairs and soon Dr. Goldstein came to them. Tommy was introduced to him, then he led them to the desk and admitted Jeanine as a patient. He went with them to her room.

"Don't forget to see Dr. Cardwell Monday morning to get

the radium needles put in. I'll be checking on you. Glad to have met you, young man." He shook hands with Tommy and left. Jan and Jeanine sat on the bed. Aunt Maggie took the chair and Tommy sat on the window sill. No one wanted to mention why they were there, yet it was quite obvious. Tommy grabbed the bell and put it to his mouth like a microphone.

"If you will just look this way ladies, you will see that this is our most luxurious suite." They smiled at him and he went on. "First of all this room comes completely equipped with all kinds of interesting gadgets. As you see, I'm holding in my hand a bell. This bell is quite useful for calling nurses when you need a piece of cotton or a tooth pick to clean out your ears, or other obvious reasons. Up on the wall you will notice a very new model TV complete with a remote control. There's a wonderfully firm bed," he demonstrated by pushing down on the mattress a few times. "But best of all, this room comes equipped with a bed table so you can have your breakfast, or all your meals in bed if you so desire. Thank you for your kind attention ladies, that ends the discourse for this tour." Jan gave him a gentle shove.

"You're crazy as a loon, Tommy, but I like you anyway," Jeanine smiled, then added, "now I want you all to go home. I'll be perfectly all right. You can come back at visiting hours tomorrow. When I'll really need you is Monday morning. I don't know anything about radium needles and even though I'm not afraid, I'd like to know Jan and Aunt Maggie are here."

"I'll be here too, Jeanine," Tommy said. He squeezed Jan's hand and said, "I hope I'm part of the family, or will be one of these days."

Jeanine looked at Jan's radiant face with a question in her eyes. Jan nodded, then exclaimed, "But not until you're well, Jeanine. I need you for my Maid of Honor." She held up her hand to show off her lovely diamond.

"Then that settles it. I promise you, I'll be that Maid of Honor, toothless or not. Now scoot, all of you and I'll look for you tomorrow. Your ring is beautiful, Jan. Congratulations to you both."

After they left, Jeanine got ready for bed, hanging her things in the closet, wondering just how strong her faith was. She wouldn't even say the word "cancer." Before she got into bed she dug in the bottom of her suitcase and found the manila folder marked "Dr. Ben." Inside were all the letters she had received from him. She climbed into bed, propped herself up with the pillows at her back. She opened the folder and took out the very first letter and read it. There it was . . . the word, "Ladybug." She thought she knew what a ladybug was but had looked it up in the dictionary to get it's exact meaning and it said: "A small insect. In the early stages they are encased in larvae (or a sort of cocoon). They receive their name from their graceful form and delicate coloring." Had he guessed she was a woman? She went to his next letter and on through six months of weekly epistles until she came to that last one. Lying back on the pillows she let a tear fall before she wiped it away. She liked what he liked and felt he was the kind of person it would be easy to know. Why had she waited so long to tell him who she really was. Maybe it wasn't meant to be.

Going back over the afternoon in her mind, she smiled at Tommy's antics, trying so desperately to make her feel better when it was really Aunt Maggie and Jan who needed cheering. She knew how worried they were about her and wished she could transfer some of her tranquility to them.

Sunday afternoon she had quite a few visitors, including Mr. Hart and Pastor Webb. Before he left he took her hand and prayed with her.

"Jeanine," he said pleasantly, "you won't be out of our thoughts. The whole church will be praying for you, and I'll be here during the operation with Jan and your Aunt." He

57

squeezed her hand and left.

Mr. Hart didn't know what to say and stood around awkwardly, twisting his felt hat in his hands.

"I told you how enthused the buyer at that Christian store was about your 'Cherubs' lines, didn't I?"

"Yes, Mr. Hart, and Jan and I have finished a lot more to take care of my time in the hospital. She'll be bringng them to you soon."

"Well then, guess I'll be going." He went over to the bed and gently touched her arm. "I'll be praying."

"Thank you. That's what I'll need a lot of."

Tommy and Jan came in with Aunt Maggie. Tommy had a large stuffed Snoopy dog in his arms. He came over to her bed, leaned down and kissed her on the cheek.

"Here you are, sis, thought you needed a guardian and here he is. He's to keep an eye on you when we can't."

"Tommy, he's great and what a thoughtful thing to do." Jeanine gave Snoopy a hug and sat him up at the foot of her bed.

Jan gave her Emily Bronte's *Wuthering Heights* she'd started reading in Chicago. Maybe she'd have time in the hospital to finish it.

Aunt Maggie hugged her tight when they left at the end of visiting hours.

"We'll be here bright and early in the morning," Jan said as she gave her a hug and kiss. Tommy squeezed her hand tight. They had such worried looks she wanted to shout, "Everything's going to be fine, just wait and see."

Monday morning dawned bright and beautiful for a winter day. It had snowed during the night and the world looked clean and sparkly. Jan and Aunt Maggie came early but no one came to get Jeanine, so she slipped on her robe and went to the nurses desk on her floor to ask where she could find Dr. Cardwell. She was told his office was on the fifth floor, so they walked down the steps. There was no one in his office so she didn't know anything else to do but go in and sit on the examining table. Soon Dr. Cardwell came in and introduced himself and met Jan and Aunt Maggie. He turned to Jeanine.

"Jeanine Page, I presume. Are you afraid?"

"No. Just wishing for a miracle, I guess." Jeanine smiled thinking, if He wanted to, God could just make the tumor vanish.

"Well, maybe this will help." He looked in her mouth, then said, "I don't see any reason to wait do you? Let's go get those needles in." He was so cheerful it was like it was no big deal. Jan and Aunt Maggie were sent to the waiting room and told they would be called. Then he took Jeanine to a room where the table was in the middle. She was told to lie on the table and he spread a blanket over her up to her neck. Immediately it seemed the room was full of nurses and interns to watch the procedure. For a moment Jeanine couldn't understand all the people being there, then she remembered Vanderbilt was a teaching hospital and these would-be doctors and nurses had to see this kind of procedure to know how it was done.

She had thought she would be put to sleep, but Dr. Cardwell just squirted some foam in her mouth and waited a few minutes. She closed her eyes so she couldn't see all those people staring at her. For a moment she raised her thoughts to the Lord. "Thank you, Lord, for what you are going to do through these needles."

"Okay." It was Dr. Cardwell and he was all business. "It's time to start." It seemed to Jeanine that Dr. Cardwell was standing high above her, pushing hard to get each needle through her tongue and into the tumor.

At one time, Dr. Goldstein had told her to take her finger and feel the tumor under her tongue. When she did, in her mind's eye it was as hard as a rock and seemed like an avocado seed. And now needles were being pushed into it.

Several times she heard Dr. Cardwell say to the gallery, "I've never had a patient like this." She had no idea what other patients did, but she thought, "Thank you, Lord."

Six needles were put in and the threads were taped to the left side of her face. Then x-rays were made to make sure the needles were in the tumor. After that she was wheeled to a private room and told to drink a glass of water every hour because of the radium.

Aunt Maggie and Jan were brought to her room to sit with her.

A nurse brought in a glass and pitcher of water filled with ice.

"Don't forget to drink a glass every hour. Okay?"

Jeanine nodded feeling quite miserable with a mouth full of needles that stuck up above her tongue.

After an hour Jan gave her a glass of water, but it ran out of the corners of her mouth as her tongue was beginning to swell.

Since she couldn't talk she motioned for a pen and paper and wrote, "Give me a wash rag with ice in it. I can't swallow." So she sucked on an ice rag most of the time.

Tuesday Dr. Cardwell came in looking worried.

"I don't understand what's happening here," he said. "You don't have a fever and you have no infection, yet your tongue is swelling too much. I've put as many as twenty-five needles in a person's tongue and it never swelled like this."

Jeanine asked for her tablet and smiled as she wrote on it, "I have an intercessor." Whether Dr. Cardwell understood what she meant she didn't know, but she had turned her body and this whole situation over to Him and she felt whatever was happening was His doing.

By late afternoon she heard noises in the hall like some kind of equipment being moved near her room. Dr. Cardwell came in and asked Jan if she could stay all night and she agreed. Plainly Dr. Cardwell was planning to do a tracheostomy on her, but she felt so strongly that God was doing something, she wrote on her tablet, "You don't need to stay. They will not be using that equipment on me tonight. I know God is doing something. Go home and get your rest and come back early tomorrow. Trust me with Him."

Some of Jeanine's faith was rubbing off on Jan for she agreed to go and Tommy took her home.

Jeanine spent a restless, uncomfortable night after a nurse gave her a penicillin pill instead of a shot and the pill got stuck in front of one of the needles and just had to stay there until it melted. It was quite bitter, but there was no need for that equipment that night.

She got so good at writing notes that one day Tommy came with a child's slate and that was much better than the tablet. She even wrote jokes and they marveled at her good spirits.

Sometimes the strings got loose from the side of her face and slipped down her throat making her gag until she could ring for a nurse.

On Wednesday, Dr. Goldstein came to see her, patting her arm. "You're a good patient I hear, but your tongue is too swollen for me to operate on Friday so we're going to leave the needles in another twenty-four hours. Dr. Cardwell will take them out on Friday. Do you understand?" She nodded. He patted her arm. "Good girl." "God wants those needles in twenty-four more hours to shrink the tumor more," she thought and was happy He was in charge.

Friday came. It was Aunt Maggie's day to volunteer. She brought her rolling library in to see if there was something Jeanine wanted to look at, but she was obviously too miserable, so she gave her a hug and continued on her rounds.

In the afternoon Dr. Cardwell came with a table to move her to his operating room to take the needles out. It was a great relief but her tongue was quite unmanageable so she kept the slate handy. She was moved to a semi-private room. Jan and Aunt Maggie moved her things and she made sure her folder of letters was with her clothes. Dr. Ben was always in the back of her mind.

On Tuesday night the lady anesthetist came to tell her what she was going to use to put her to sleep and to assure her that everything that could be done for her was being done. The operation was scheduled for 8:00 A.M. Wednesday morning.

That night when all her visitors had gone, she went to her bathroom and looked in the mirror. Trying to remember what all Dr. Goldstein had said he was going to do. She wondered what she would look like. "Maybe I'll be so deformed Dr. Ben wouldn't want me, even if we met."

"Lord, if you could just sort of pour yourself into my body some way, I know that wherever your body touched mine I'd be healed. I leave myself in your hands and thank you for what you are going to do."

When the nurse came in later to give her a sleeping pill she declined. "I won't need it," she said confidently, and she didn't.

Bright and early the next morning a nurse came in to give her a shot. Her pastor came and had a brief prayer with her. Jan, Aunt Maggie and Tommy came only minutes before she was to be wheeled out. They hugged her, assured her of their love and prayers. Then she was wheeled out and almost asleep by the time she got to the operating room.

"Jeanine, can you hear me?" It seemed to come from far away. With a great deal of effort she barely opened her eyes and saw Dr. Goldstein smile.

"You're going to do fine," he said and she heard no more.

Chapter 7

A great mist was all around her and she coughed, but she seemed to be in a deep, deep well, held by an invisible hand. The hand squeezed hers and a deep voice said, "You're doing fine, little Ladybug." She drifted off again. Much later the mist seemed to be all around still and she coughed again.

"Jeanine, it's Jan. Just wanted you to know I'm here and so is Tommy." She felt her hand being squeezed as she went out again.

Still later in the night the mist was still there and she seemed not to have left the deep well. She sensed, rather than saw, someone near. A deep, resonant voice spoke to her assuringly, "You're not alone, Jeanine. I'm going to stay with you." Her hand was being lifted and held in a large, warm strong hand.

The mist made her cough but she felt wonderful with her hand in that man's hand. Somehow she knew it was a man's hand, 'though her eyelids were too heavy to open, then she was gone again.

As she drifted in and out of consciousness that presence was there holding her hand and even though she was still in the mist she wasn't afraid. Something was making her cough a lot and it hurt each time. Once she felt as though the presence had moved and was standing by her bed gently caressing her forehead. It felt so good she wanted to tell him not to stop but she couldn't seem to open her mouth or her eyes before she was gone again.

One last time she finally opened her eyes for one minute and looked up into his face. The mist swirled about her and she coughed, but as she drifted off again she thought, "It's Dr. Ben. How wonderful."

All day Thursday she slept, not knowing who came or went, or that by late afternoon she was moved to her room, or that her family was there in case she should come to. But she never woke up until Friday morning, her time in Intensive Care almost blotted out by the present.

Her head felt like she had a football helmet on and now that she was fully awake, Dr. Goldstein came in and unwrapped her head, assuring her that the operation went as planned, with no complications and she should heal nicely. After he left she wanted so badly to look in a mirror and yet she was afraid of what she would see. Did she have any chin left? Finally she had to see herself, so she rang for a nurse to bring her a mirror.

She took one look and burst out laughing. There were so many stitches, from ear to ear and through her lip and down her neck, a nose tube for feeding and a tube in either side of her neck for drainage, and I.V. in one arm and a tracheostomy tube.

"What's so funny?" the nurse asked incredulously.

"I look just like Raggedy Ann," she wrote on her slate. The nurse just smiled.

Quick as a flash a rhyme came to Jeanine and as soon as the nurse left she wrote it down on her slate:

> Here I lie on my hospital bed.
> Tubes in my arm and tubes in my head:
> A hole in my neck and stitches all over
> If I got disconnected,
> I'd be sleeping in clover.

Jan and Aunt Maggie and Tommy came at visiting hours. They laughed with her, but they were not prepared for Dr. Goldstein's reaction. When he read Jeanine's rhyme, he laughed until the tears rolled down his cheeks. Jeanine guessed he wasn't expecting anything silly from a cancer patient.

Just then a white coated figure appeared in the doorway. When Jeanine saw him her heart leaped. It was Dr. Ben, but how?

Dr. Goldstein turned to the newcomer, went to greet him then brought him to Jeanine's bed.

"Jeanine, this is Dr. William Rensalear, our resident psychologist. Sometimes cancer patients need his help, but Dr.," he turned to look at him, "I'm not sure this patient does. Look at this." He showed Dr. Rensalear her rhyme. What a hearty laugh he had but how could he not be Dr. Ben when he looked so much like the man she conjured up in her mind so long ago. How handsome he was in real life, much more than the man she imagined.

Dr. Goldstein was still laughing and wiping his eyes. "Jeanine," he said, "may I put this rhyme in your record." She nodded and he left the room still chuckling. She'd write it down later.

Tommy came around and slapped the doctor on the back. To Jeanine's astonishment, Tommy said, "Jeanine, this is my young brother, Will, I told you about. He never wanted me to tell anyone he was a doctor, but now you know."

Dr. Will took Jeanine's hand and looked into her eyes with those clear brown eyes she'd imagined for Dr. Ben.

"I'm on call anytime you need me. Just tell a nurse and I'll be at your side." His deep voice was just how she thought Dr. Ben would sound.

She still had the mist flowing up under her chin but now Dr. Rensalear told her it was necessary for anyone who has had a tracheostomy to make them cough so they won't catch pneumonia.

So this was Will, Tommy's brother. What a disappointment that her imagination should conjure up a neighbor, 'though a nice one. Maybe that's why she imagined him looking as he did. She'd probably seen him in her Dad's stargazer sometime. Will's hair was brown and wavy just as she imagined. He was tall and broad shouldered. He looked solid too, where Tommy was all muscle. She wrote on her slate, "Thank you for coming. Glad to meet you." She gave him a smile, as much as she could under the circumstances.

"I'll be back," he said, returning her smile. "Can't neglect my patients." Then he waved as Tommy walked him to the door. From the way he greeted Jan, Jeanine realized they knew each another.

After visiting hours when Jan, Tommy and Aunt Maggie had left, the nurse came in to settle Jeanine down for the night. Jeanine refused the sleeping pill and the pain pill. She guessed the Lord had done what she asked Him to for her mouth did not give her any pain. She was about to turn off her light when the door opened to her surprise. Dr. Rensalear came in the room and over to her bed. He picked up her wrist and held it, searching her face.

"Just checking on my patient." He gave her a dazzling smile. "I have an advantage over you. I can talk all I want and you can't answer." He looked at his watch, checking her pulse.

Jeanine grabbed up her slate and with a gleam in her eyes wrote quickly then held it up to him. "Oh, yes I can. Try me."

He caught her gaiety.

"Okay. How old are you?" he asked, grinning.

"24. Why?"

"I can't treat you if I don't have all the facts. Are you married?"

"No. What kind of 3rd degree is this?"

"For future reference, in case you are my patient again." The corners of his mouth were trying to turn up and he was having a time keeping a straight face.

"I hope I never need a psychiatrist, or whatever you are."

"Ouch!" he exclaimed. "Maybe I need to take lessons from you."

"Glad to teach you anytime." She erased that and wrote, "Turn about is fair play, right?"

He nodded. She erased her words and wrote, "How old are you?"

He smiled and answered, "28."

She wrote again, "Are you married?"

"No," he answered, smiled again and said thoughtfully, "Jeanine Page, you're really something. Good night." He walked to the door, turned and waved as he went out.

She turned out the light, smiling to herself. He might not be so bad after all. Then she remembered Bob Stillman and sighed.

Every day she gained her strength and the nurses and all her doctors, the young interns who drained and cleaned her tubes, were talking about the patient in room #661, a cancer patient who wrote silly poems and made jokes, who kept tracts on her bedside table and handed them to nurses, nurses' aides, or anyone who came to see her. Some of the nurses even came and got some to take to other patients.

She still had to write notes until Dr. Goldstein took the stitches out of her mouth and removed the "trach." He had already removed some of the stitches from her neck, but as long as the "trach" was in her throat she couldn't make a sound.

One evening she heard voices and footsteps approaching her curtained bed. Dr. Goldstein often brought young interns to show them what he'd done to her mouth. She heard him say, "This is the most phlegmatic young woman I've ever known." For a moment she wondered about his statement, then remembered that phlegmatic meant calm or peaceful. "Thank you, Lord." She prayed in her heart before Dr. Goldstein opened the curtain and introduced her to the six young men. Then he asked her to open her mouth wide while each of the young men, using a small flashlight, examined her mouth.

She was able to be up some every day. Her room was in a new round section of the hospital so she pushed her intravenous feeding pole as she walked around the circle of rooms. She stopped before each room and said a little prayer for whoever that patient was. One day, Dr. Rensalear came out of one of the rooms and saw her standing there with her curly head bowed.

"Jeanine," he said anxiously, "are you all right?" She looked so tiny and defenseless with that nose tube still hanging from her nose and he remembered one time she had laughed, pointed to her nose tube and wrote on her slate, "I feel like an elephant," never a complaint about it but what a sense of humor.

Jeanine carried her slate with her and wrote on it, "I was just praying for that patient. He may not have anyone praying for him."

"Ah, Jeanine," Dr. Will sighed. "You're going to be fine. I'll see you tonight." He lifted his hand like he might touch her face, then dropped it. As she watched him go into another room somewhere back in her memory something was trying to come to her about what he'd just said, "You're going to be fine." Someone said that to her before, but when and where?

Dr. Rensalear had started coming to her room regularly after visiting hours, saying he was "treating" her, but he talked about what he'd like to do and many things unrelated to the treatment of cancer. Sometimes she wrote some things on her slate, sometimes she'd ask him questions and he'd answer, but she felt he could relax with her and it was a rest from his daily routine to be there, just visiting. Sometimes he read to her. She loved his "treatments" and waited eagerly each night for his visit.

This night she was ready for him. On her slate she wrote, "Read to me from the Bible, John 14, the first ten verses." She'd forgotten her folder of Dr. Ben's letters was on the table and her Bible was on top. She noticed him glance at it, then sat down and began to read. When he came to verse six, "I am the way, the truth, and the life, no man cometh unto the Father but by me," he closed the Bible but held his place.

"You believe this to be God's Word, don't you?" She nodded.

"That Jesus is God's Son and no one can get to heaven except through Jesus. In other words, believing in Him?" She nodded her black curls. Oh how she wanted to be able to tell him what Jesus meant to her. He opened the Bible and read the rest of the verses. Then he closed the Bible and returned it to the table. Turning back to her, he picked up her hand and squeezed it lightly.

"You've given me some things to think about tonight. Sleep tight. Good night." He flicked off the light and left her in a quandery, still feeling the warmth of his hand on hers. She raised her hand to her lips, wondering what it would be like to have his lips on hers. She shivered with delight, then gasped as her own boldness. "Whatever am I thinking of. I'm just a patient to him."

She flicked the light back on, took the folder of Dr. Ben's letters and read the last one again. Then put the folder on the table and turned out the light. "Oh, Dr. Ben. I haven't even got a face for you anymore, but I still want to know you and I still want you to know Jesus." She closed her eyes and fell asleep with a prayer on her lips for Dr. Ben.

The next day was her twenty-fifth birthday. She awoke with a happy feeling of anticipation, for what she didn't know, except that she had finally reached the quarter century mark in her life and that should count for something.

About 10:00 o'clock, all her nurses and doctors, including Dr. Goldstein came in with a cake and candles and sang "Happy Birthday," then clapped their hands. She quickly wrote on her slate, "Thank you all. Do you usually do this for your patients who have birthdays?" They answered, "No, but you're a special patient. You can't eat this, but your family can enjoy it."

They told her to make a wish and then blow out the candles. Her wish was for Dr. Ben, of course, and then she tried to blow out the candles but couldn't form her mouth to blow, so all those who were close enough blew them out for her. The nurses all came and gave her a hug and kiss and a personal "Happy Birthday" and wishes for complete recovery. The young interns all shook her hand and one said, "You are a joy to know." Last of all Dr. Goldstein took her hand and wished her many more years of health and happiness. He spoke encouragingly, "You're making such good progress that we're going to stop the I.V.'s and start feeding you by your nose tube." They all filed out waving and smiling. She waved back feeling good inside.

That noon a nurse came in to start her nose feedings with a milky white substance. She held the tube up and poured a small container full into the tube, but it was ice cold and the minute it hit her stomach it came right back up. Jeanine had had nothing in her stomach for two and one-half weeks and it wasn't ready for something ice cold. She wrote on her slate, "If you could heat it, I think I could keep it down." The nurse took it away and soon returned. This time she was able to keep the warm substance down. From then on they heated it each time.

That afternoon when Tommy brought her family, they came loaded down with gifts and cards. Joan and Jennifer had gone together and gotten her a clock radio to put by her bed, accompanied by pretty birthday cards with lovely verses for their sister.

Jan put her gift in her lap as she sat propped up with pillows, and said, "Here, open mine next." After she had Tommy cut the tape with his pocket knife, she opened the box to find a sheer pink gown and a short bed jacket to match, with ruffles around the neck and wrists. Jeanine wrote, "It's beautiful and as soon as I open these other gifts I'm going to make Tommy leave so I can put it on."

Next Aunt Maggie put her box on her lap and she also had given her a pretty blue gown and jacket with lace and ribbons. There was also a pale blue satin ribbon to put around her head.

"It's so hard to look pretty in bed all the time, so I thought the ribbon in your curls would help." Jeanine held her arms out to Jan and her Aunt and squeezed them hard, with tears in her eyes, then she wrote again, "I love you so much. Thank you. I can't help but look pretty now. I'll write Joan and Jennifer and thank them."

"Don't leave me out," Tommy exclaimed, coming over to her bed and dropping his small, square green foil-wrapped package in her lap. She took off the white bow and handed it to Jan, then unwrapped the box carefully. The paper was so pretty she didn't want to tear it. Inside was a jeweler's box and inside it was a shiny gold chain bracelet. Her mouth formed an "Oh," and she held it up to Jan to clasp on her wrist. She held her arm up and jiggled the bracelet.

"Thought that would help you look and feel pretty." His voice was soft as he looked at her. She grabbed her slate.

"Thank you, Tommy. I love it." She opened her arms and gave him a sisterly hug.

She made Tommy leave the room and Jan helped her into the pink gown. The jacket with the ruffles looked so stunning against her black curls that Jan and Aunt Maggie just stared and she sensed it was very becoming. They let Tommy back in the room and his eyes told her too. She picked up her slate and asked Tommy, "Why didn't you tell us your brother was so handsome, and a doctor?"

Tommy answered, "He asked us not to tell anyone. People always seem to make a lot out of the fact that he's a doctor. They find out sooner or later anyway. As far as being handsome, I'd like to say he took after me, but we're only step brothers, so I guess he got his good looks from his mother."

She wrote again, "Why doesn't he go by your name?"

"Dad wanted to adopt him, but Mom wanted him to keep the Rensalear name going, so he kept it."

They left then, saying they wouldn't be back that night, but would come the next day. After they left a nurse brought in a green vase with a half dozen deep red rose buds. Knowing she couldn't talk, the nurse took out the card and held it for her. It read, "Guess Who?" There was a question in her eyes. The nurse said, "I haven't the slightest idea who they could be from." And left the room, leaving Jeanine to gaze at the velvety petals, loving the heady perfume that filled the room.

When Dr. Rensalear came that night she saw the surprised look in his eyes at her pretty new jacket and felt good.

"Well, don't you look pretty and your eyes are so full of sparkle. What are you so happy about tonight?" He was smiling at her with that crazy way he had of turning up the corners of his mouth before the smile was complete.

She wrote, "For one thing, today is my birthday and everyone has been wonderful to me."

"Well, I have to add my birthday greetings too, so 'Happy Birthday.'" He walked over to the vase of roses and read the card. "You have a secret admirer I see." Suddenly, she knew and wrote on her slate, her eyes full of mischief, "Thank you for those beautiful roses, but why didn't you sign the card?"

He returned her look of mischief. "I wondered if you'd figure out it was me. Well, doctors don't usually send flowers to their patients and can't you guess all the buzzing and gossip that would go around if the nurses knew. I wouldn't have known about it, but Tommy was talking about what he and Jan were getting you for your birthday and I wanted to have a part because you are a very special patient." He smiled at her, then quickly turned away.

She wrote to him, "I love them. It was very thoughtful of you."

After reading her note he said, "It made me happy to get them. Now shall I read Emily Bronte tonight?" She nodded and listened to his deep voice as he read. Later, when he left she thought what a wonderful day it had been and fell asleep with the perfume of roses filling the room.

The next day Dr. Goldstein came in to check on her progress and told her if she could drink as much boullion and other such liquids as she'd been getting by nose tube, the tube could come out. So she began drinking all the juices and boullions she could, even though every swallow hurt because the "trach" was still in her throat and the nose tube still in her nose.

The interns came every day to clean her drainage tubes and "trach." She wrote funny notes, and joked with them. They seemed to enjoy taking care of her. Then one day they came and took the tubes out altogether. She felt like a bird out of a cage. Now she just had little white scars on her neck where the tubes had been.

Jan, Tommy and Aunt Maggie came every day and seemed happier about her progress than anyone.

That night when Dr. Rensalear came she was ecstatic.

"Your eyes are doing it again," he said.

"Doing what?" she wrote.

"Sparkling. What is it tonight?"

"Dr. Goldstein says if I keep drinking liquids like I did all day today, I get to quit being an elephant."

"I like elephants," he teased, "especially the kind with black curls and violet eyes and blue ribbons in their hair."

"But wouldn't the nose keep getting in the way of . . . " she started to write "kisses," then shocked at her thoughts she grabbed her eraser rag to wipe the slate clean, but he quickly took the slate from her and read her unfinished question and guessed what she had been going to write.

"You're right," he teased again, "it would." He seemed to sense her embarrassment and took the rag himself and wiped the words off the slate.

"There." He held it up for her to see. "It's clean and forgotten. Feel better?" She blushed and nodded.

"Okay." He was still smiling at her unfinished question. "It's time for me to read to you. After all I am a psychiatrist and I'm supposed to be helping you get over your fear of your cancer." He pulled a chair up by her bed and sat down.

"But I'm not afraid and never have been," she wrote.

"I know. That's what's so amazing to me and all the others who have treated and worked with you each day. You're always so happy and cheerful. Just tell me why? Cancer is a frightening word." She answered as fast as she could write.

"God is using me to prove He can take care of cancer so I can tell a friend of mine so he will believe in Him too." Dr. Will read her slate and was silent a long time, not looking at her.

"You really believe this don't you?"

"With all my heart," she wrote. "God can be trusted."

"I know," he said softly. "I trusted Him with my life too." Hearing him say that tears popped into her eyes, but a huge grin spread across her face.

She grabbed her slate and wrote, "Wonderful! When?"

"Last night when I went home. I couldn't sleep for

74

thinking of all those scriptures I read to you the other night. I guess He wouldn't let go of me until I yielded." Without thinking, Jeanine held out her arms to welcome another child into God's family. Not understanding her completely innocent gesture, he grasped her and held her close to him.

"Ah, Jeanine, Jeanine." He held her away from him to look into her eyes but when he noticed the questioning look there he laid her back on the pillows and stood a little away from the bed.

"This-a-person you speak of. Does he know what you've been through or what you're trying to prove to him?"

Her trusty slate came up and she wrote, "Not yet. But someday I'll tell him." She erased that and wrote, "Now I'm ready to hear some more from *Wuthering Heights,* please." He looked at his watch and said, almost sadly, "I'm afraid I can't stay any longer tonight. I have something I need to do now." He looked at her a long time, then smiled that smile that always did things to her stomach.

"Don't go away. I may need to see you again." Then he hurried out of the room leaving Jeanine puzzled. She could have kicked herself for her recent actions. When she held out her arms to him, she was only welcoming another child of God, but the minute his arms were around her, those feelings vanished and she wanted him to keep holding her close. He smelled of antiseptics, but his uniform smelled like it had been freshly washed and dried in the sun. He did seem to be different from Bob Stillman.

Thinking again of those few minutes in his arms, she was aware of wonderful sensations and a swiftly beating heart. Why did he leave so suddenly? She had probably frightened him away. Just when she was beginning to have wonderful feelings about him and anticipated the evenings when he came to her room for her "treatment." She'd try to make it up to him the next night.

She remembered Dr. Goldstein's visit earlier that night

when he'd said, "If you keep improving like this, you can go home on Saturday." So she had kept up drinking the juices and boullions.

Thursday morning when he came, he took out the nose tube. Then she walked down the hall to a treatment room and sat on a table while he took the "trach" out of her throat. He let her look in a mirror at the perfectly round hole in her neck. What an amazing thing it was to see that hole. Without anything over it she couldn't make a sound, but when he put a bandaid over it, she could talk. What a joy that was . . . no more writing notes. He took the stitches out of her tongue. He said the hole in her neck needed no stitches, that it would heal itself and she thought what a miracle was the human body, to be able to go through so much and heal itself.

The rest of that day she kept drinking liquids and even slurped some jello. It was so great to be able to talk and not have to write. It would be great to talk to Dr. Rensalear when he came that night. She was getting more restless waiting for that time to come.

When Tommy brought Jan and Aunt Maggie at visiting time, they were so happy that she could talk to them. It was a joyous visit and they were anticipating the day she could come home.

That night Dr. Goldstein came back and told her she had done so well that day that she could go home on Friday instead of Saturday. He said proudly, "You are, without a doubt, the best patient I've ever had." She tried to make him understand it was the Lord who gave her the faith to see her through.

All evening she waited and waited but Dr Rensalear never came to her room. She finally realized he wasn't coming and since she would be leaving the next morning, she'd probably never see him again. Some tears slipped slowly from her eyes in the dark. Again she had done something that made someone she liked very much leave and not come back. She hadn't realized how very much she'd grown to depend on the evenings when he came or how happy he'd made her. Even if they lived one-half mile across the river from each other, he probably would never come over. After all, hadn't he said she was just a patient, and a toothless one at that. She turned her face to the wall and cried herself to sleep.

Tommy, Jan and Aunt Maggie were there at 9:00 to help her pack up. She rang for a nurse and asked about Dr. Rensalear, forgetting for a minute that he was Tommy's brother. She thought she wanted to see him for just a minute to say goodbye. The nurse said he wrote on her chart that she didn't need to see a psychiatrist any more. The nurse added that he had a clinic in town and only came to the hospital when they called him. Jeanine looked at Tommy then with a question in her eyes.

"Will you tell him how much his treaments helped me, Tommy?" He nodded.

The nurses who had become friends came to say goodbye. One very black, very round and very cheerful nurse gave her a bear hug and exclaimed, "You are the toppest most patient we ever had in this here circle."

Then she was ready to be wheeled out to her old Chevy. Tommy drove to their house and she realized it was Valentine's Day.

Chapter 8

Tommy stopped at the mail box and Jan got the mail. There were Valentine cards from Joan and Jennifer and a long envelope with the newspaper logo on it. Because of what Jeanine had been through Jan handed it to her without teasing.

"Now, Jeanine, Honey," Aunt Maggie's voice was concerned. "You need to go right to bed. We don't want you tiring yourself out." Jeanine didn't need any prodding. She walked slowly up the stairs and to her room. What in the world would Dr. Ben be writing her for? But her heart pounded as she opened the envelope and took out the letter.

> Dear B.J.,
>   I know it's been awhile since I last wrote and asked why you had stopped writing, but your letters had meant so much to me I'm trying one more time.
>   Please start writing again. I miss the rapport we had and believe it or not, I'm beginning to take your God seriously.
>   Your faithful servant,
>   Dr. Ben

Maybe Dr. Ben was the answer after all. She guessed she'd answer his letter. After all, what other fun did she have, and how else was he to know about the Lord unless she wrote to him. She'd just have to conjure up another face.

So she got out her typing paper and typed the simple details of her cancer ordeal, stressing how the Lord had given her the faith to get through the ordeal without fear. She mentioned she would be going to the dentist soon to see about getting some teeth.

On her first visit to the dentist Dr. Goldsten had recommended, saying he hoped the dentist could make teeth that could hook onto the teeth that were left, her hopes were dashed following the examination.

"You have no gums, my dear. I couldn't possibly make you dentures as you have nothing to put them on. However, I do know an orthodontist at Vanderbilt and he makes gums. So, when you have your gums, come back and see me." He gave her the doctor's name.

What a disappointment. It was hard not being able to take a bite out of anything and to always use a fork and put her food between the two teeth she had left, and eating took so much longer because she had to take such little bites. But there was hope if she could have the gums made.

She looked up the orthodontist and after examining her mouth, he saw what had been done and complimented Dr. Goldstein on a fantastic job. With her tongue shortened and tied down on one side, he thought she talked very well. She only had trouble with certain sounds where her tongue needed to touch her teeth to pronounce them and it didn't, but she was working on them. He was ready to make an appointment for her to have the gums made in March. However, she was disappointed again when Dr. Goldstein said, "Not yet." She guessed it was only natural for him to be sure the cancer was not coming back, but she already knew the answer to that. God had answered her prayers and brought her through this and He wasn't going to let her go without teeth to eat with and not be a complete person again, but she had to listen to Dr. Goldstein so she would wait. She couldn't lick her lips either and had to use a lip balm quite often, but that was better than dry lips and she thanked the Lord over and over for answering her prayers.

"Cherubs" was so successful she and Jan couldn't believe their good luck. It kept them busy keeping up with the demand.

Jan and Tommy were making plans for their wedding which was set for early June. Of course Tommy wanted Dr. Rensalear to be best man and Jan wanted Jeanine to be Maid of Honor. Jeanine wondered if there were any way she could gracefully get out of it. Seeing him again and having to be paired off with him would be hard. She felt she couldn't face him again after she felt she had thrown herself at him in the hospital by opening her arms to him. But she often thought of his brown eyes and the way he had looked at her so many times, his waves, just as she imagined him and his teeth so white and even. She could still hear his deep, wonderful voice. Her "treatments" had certainly been unusual to say the least and she sometimes even longed to be a patient again. He did say he had accepted the Lord and she was glad for that.

The days slipped by one by one and the day of the wedding was fast approaching. Still she could think of nothing that would take her away. Joan and Jennifer were both going to be bridesmaids, so she couldn't go to see them. She'd just have to tough it out. One thing she was thankful for, her teeth that were left kept her from looking like a little old granny and she kept her tongue at the bottom of her mouth all the time so her mouth was not sunk in like most people with no bottom teeth.

She went with Jan to pick out her wedding dress and the dresses for herself, Joan and Jennifer and they had a lot of fun. When Jan tried on the dress and put the veil on over her raven tresses, Jeanine thought she looked just beautiful and knew she would be the prettiest June bride ever.

Jan wanted to be married in Aunt Maggie's garden, so

Aunt Maggie was beside herself making all kinds of plans for the wedding. Of course she felt Jan could not be married without an arch, decorated with vines and greenery and there were tables to be prepared for guests, one for the Guest Book and another for the cake and refreshments.

One day after helping Aung Maggie work on invitations, Jeanine walked down the long lane to the mail box. She hadn't heard from Dr. Ben since she'd written him about her operation and she felt quite let down that he had never written at all. After all his letters had meant to her, she guessed she had been wrong in thinking her letters had meant something to him.

She opened the mail box and the first thing she saw was that long white envelope with the newspaper logo in the return address. She practically ran back to the house and up to her room, to her favorite place for reading his letters, the middle of her bed, and opened his letter with trembling fingers.

Dear B.J.,

Sorry to be so late in answering your very shocking letter about your operation. I have been out of town for several months on a lecture tour and just read your letter.

I am stunned and hurt that you went through that terrible ordeal and never wrote me. I thought we had become close friends and close friends confide in each other.

But of course you thought I would laugh at your confidence in your God. I told you in my last letter that I was beginning to take your God seriously. Believe it or not, after getting your letter I even prayed for you.

I believe we've been corresponding long enough and now it's time we met. Don't you agree? I'm sure we'll know each other.

If you care to meet me, please be at *The Blue Circle Restaurant* at 7:00 P.M. on Thursday, May 3rd.

I'm looking forward very much to meeting you and seeing you in person at last.

Your faithful servant,
Dr. Ben

Unbelievable! Dr. Ben wanted to meet her and he had prayed for her. "Oh, thank you, Lord. It won't be hard to introduce him to You now. He needs You so much, although I must admit, his articles have been much more to my liking lately."

Jan called her to dinner and she ran down the steps more spritely than ususal. Jan and Aunt Maggie looked at her questioningly.

"Guess what? Dr. Ben wants to meet me after all this time."

"When?" Jan asked. Aunt Maggie asked the blessing and began passing food. By now Jeanine had grown used to eating small portions of everything, especially meat. Eating on two teeth always took longer for each bite.

"Next Thursday. That's day after tomorrow, at *The Blue Circle Restaurant.* Do you know where that is?"

"No. But I'm sure Tommy will know. He's coming over tonight and we can ask him."

"Jan, I want to look as lovely as possible. Could you go with me out to Hickory Hollow to Botony and Lowes Department store and help me find something soft and feminine. I don't want to look sporty for this dinner." She paused and held her fork in the air. "Oh my goodness, what about my hair? Maybe I'll get a long, shiny black wig as glamorous as your hair. " Her thoughts raced on and on.

"Of course I'll go with you. It should be fun."

Jeanine was in another world as she exclaimed, "I wonder what he looks like and how will I know him? If I see a good looking man looking like he's looking for someone, I guess that will be him."

Jan laughed. "You're in a tizzy again. Don't worry. When you leave here Thursday, you'll look good enough to eat."

That night she slipped in and out of sleep, dreaming about meeting a faceless man. When Tommy had come over and Jan had told him about her date, he had assured her they would see she got there on time if she and Jan motored over to his house then he could take them in his car. He had never driven the long way around to their house. It was much easier to cross the river.

The next day they gave themselves plenty of time for the long drive to Hickory Hollow Mall and parked in front of Botony and Lowes. When they got inside, Jan remarked, "First the blouses. Then we'll look at dresses to see if you would look more feminine in a soft flowing faille." Jeanine had found the blouse rack and picked out one she liked, held it up and called to Jan at another rack.

"Look Jan, how about this? It was a blouse of soft pink pongee with a foldover collar, long billowy sleeves caught at the wrists in a band and fastened with a pink pearl button. "A strand of pink pearls would be feminine and flattering. What do you think?"

"Hold onto it. Let's see what kind of a skirt would look great. I believe a white pleated skirt like this would be just the thing." She held up a white skirt on a hanger.

"I love it already!" Jeanine exclaimed. "Let's find the pearls to go with it." She wore petite sizes in everything and they soon made those three purchases.

"Now the wig." Jeanine's eyes were shining.

"Do you really think you want to wear a wig?"

"I want to look as glamorous as you do." She looked at her sister enviously.

"But maybe Dr. Ben would rather you look your natural self," Jan reminded.

"With my short hair? That's okay for sports, but not for glamour."

They found a wiggery and Jeanine started trying on wigs but her head was so small most of them were too big. Finally, the sales lady went to her display window and came back with a shiny, black wig of straight shoulder length hair with feathery bangs just like Jan's. The minute the lady fit it on her head and she looked in the mirror, she didn't recognize herself. She looked almost like Jan and just as pretty.

"Oh, Jan, look at me!"

"Umm," Jan mumbled and looked at her from all angles. "You really think you want to wear it and will feel right in it?" Jan questioned.

"I feel almost like a belle at a ball."

"But this is not a masquerade, Jeanine."

"I still want it. Yes, I'll take it."

As they were walking out with their purchases, Jan asked, "Did it ever occur to you that Dr. Ben might be expecting a fellow. Remember, you said you signed your name, B.J."

"Then tomorrow night he'll find out differently, won't he? I hope he won't be disappointed," Jeanine said as they got into the car.

It had been a long day. Shopping always made her tired, and this day made her more tired with the excitement building up inside. When she got home she fixed herself a shake, which was easier than trying to eat on her fluttery stomach and went up to her room.

She hung her blouse on a hanger, twisted the hook and hung it over the door, hung the pink pearls around the hanger, hung her skirt on the door knob, then put the black wig on the styrofoam head form she'd purchased especially for that purpose, and set it on her vanity. She then laid down to rest and looked at her treasures. She dreamed about the upcoming meeting. If she could only put a face to Dr. Ben.

Suddenly, she jumped up and pulled out a drawer of her desk. Taking the folder of Dr. Ben's letters, she plopped herself in the middle of her bed and sipped her shake, reading each letter from the first to the last. As she read, she got more excited with each letter, thinking of what attracted her to the writer. He was certainly intelligent and in a debate could probably reason her right into his arms. She gasped at her thought and giggled. He seemed to be a thoughtful, caring person. He really seemed hurt that she hadn't cared enough to share the most serious thing in her life with him. Could he have been worried about her? But he didn't know she was a "she." Oh dear. She was so mixed up and suddenly she didn't even want to meet him. She enjoyed his letters. Why couldn't they just let things be as they were. No. She knew there had to be a meeting.

The next afternoon she bathed in a luxury of bubbles, dried herself with a fluffy towel then smoothed on a clean smelling body lotion. With nervous fingers she dressed, brushed some faint blusher on her face, and put on a dab of Gloria Vanderbilt perfume, a luxury she had afforded herself for this occasion. Then she called Jan to come and put on her wig. When it was in place she viewed herself in the full length mirror and sighed. The blouse and skirt were perfect together and fit her petite frame snugly but not too sensuously. The pink pearls were just right with the filmy blouse. The black wig with black patent sandals made her outfit complete and from the look in Jan's eyes, she must look passable.

"I think I look taller, don't I?" Jan smiled at her indulgently.

"Of course, sis. You've got on those pretty sandals with three inch heels. I don't see how you're going to walk in them. You're not used to anything but flats and tennis shoes."

"Don't worry. Tonight I'm going to be a perfect lady. Not a freckled faced boy. Oh, by the way, may I borrow your evening shawl and bag?" Jan produced them and they went downstairs to greet Aunt Maggie. Jeanine modeled her new outfit for her Aunt. She minced a few paces in her high heels, then twirled slowly around, letting her hair swirl around her face.

"How do you like it?" she asked anxiously.

"I don't," Aunt Maggie said firmly. Then she smiled, "You're not my little Jeanine anymore. You're a grown up woman. But you look lovely, wig and all. Go and have a wonderful time. I hope you find your Dr. Ben all that you've hoped he would be."

They walked to the top of the steps in the yard. Aunt Maggie turned on the light so they could see their way down to the pier. As they headed toward the boat Jeanine worried about getting her white skirt soiled, but Jan had been down earlier and spread towels over the seats and made sure the bottom of the boat was dry and clean. She helped Jeanine in and then got in herself to start the motor. They waved at Aunt Maggie as they pulled away.

The Bennett's pier and steps were brightly lit and Tommy was already waiting for them. He helped Jeanine out of the boat and started to pull her to him for a kiss, but Jeanine pushed him away.

"Tommy!" she laughed. "I'm Jeanine." Tommy looked at her and back at Jan, then turned to help Jan out of the boat. He gave her a hug and a long kiss. Then he turned back to Jeanine.

"Jeanine, what have you done to yourself? You are beautiful!"

"It's the wig, Tommy. I wanted to look as glamorous as Jan."

"Well, since Jan tells me this friend thinks you are a man, he's in for a big surprise. Come on let's get going." He helped them into his black Porsche and took off toward Nashville.

All during the long ride, Jan and Tommy talked about their nearing wedding day. Jeanine was glad that they had other things to occupy their minds and didn't bother her with questions or small talk. She was too busy thinking about the evening ahead and what it might mean for her future.

When Tommy got to Nashville he made so many turns she was completely lost. When he pulled up in front of the restaurant, Jeanine just sat there in the back seat, not wanting to go in.

"Well, Jeanine," Tommy said slyly, "this is the moment of truth. Shall we come back and get you around 9:30?"

Jeanine's heart was pounding so hard she could hardly hear Tommy's voice, but she answered a weak, "Yes." Jan got out and pulled her seat back, helping her sister out. Jeanine just stood there and finally Jan said, "Do you want us to go in with you?" Jeanine straightened her shoulders. "No, I've got to do this myself." They watched her until the door closed behind her and then drove off.

Jeanine stood in the ante room to one side, suddenly conscious of the scar through her lip and her toothlessness. Dr. Goldstein had done such a good job that her neck scar was sort of hidden in a small crease in her neck and was hardly noticeable. She kept noticing everyone who came in but they were all couples, or groups of people. At last! A single man! Oh, no! He was a "dotty old man" and headed right for her. What a disappointment. What would she say? When he got to her he said, "Pardon me, Miss." He hung his hat on the rack above her head, then he went into the dining area. What a relief, but she felt foolish standing there. She looked into the dining area and noticed it was very pleasant, very tastefully arranged with sparkling white table cloths and napkins and a vase of flowers in the center of each table. She guessed she'd go sit at a table. She spied an unoccupied table in a corner, a bit out of the way, and decided to sit there. She would be where she could view the people coming in and could see a single man.

As she passed a table a man touched her arm. He had on dark glasses and was dressed in a great fitting black suit, a sunshine bright white shirt with a muted red and silver tie. She turned to him.

"Pardon?" she said questioningly. He had already been served and whatever he had looked delicious, but he was looking at her strangely.

"Miss Page, is that you? Jeanine?"

"Oh, Dr. Rensalear. I'm so glad to see someone I know. I was supposed to meet someone here, but I don't know what he looks like. Would you mind if I sat with you, then I wouldn't stick out like a sore thumb."

"I wouldn't mind at all. Can I order you some tea while you're waiting. I'll even order you some fricasseed chicken like I have, or a salad."

"Well, maybe some tea and a garden salad. It takes me longer to eat now." He called the waiter over and ordered for her. He gave her an engaging smile.

"How were you able to grow your hair so long so quickly?" There was a gleam in his eyes.

"Smile if you want to. I wanted to look glamorous. You can't look glamorous in a hospital gown, can you?"

"No. I must admit you certainly do look glamorous."

"Do you really think so?"

"I do, but I really like the curls better."

"Why are you wearing those dark glasses?" she asked. He took the glasses off and showed her his left eye. It was all black and blue and yellow.

"Oh my, it's a beauty. How did it happen?"

"You won't believe this, but I ran into a door in the dark. Tommy left the closet door open in my bedroom. I should have turned on the light, but I never dreamed he'd borrow something from my closet and not close the door."

The waiter brought her salad and tea. She bowed her head for a moment to thank the Lord for her food. She opened her eyes to find him looking at her, though with those glasses she could not imagine what he was thinking.

"Dr. Rensalear . . . ." He stopped her.

"Please call me 'Will.' We're not doctor and patient now."

"That's right, we aren't are we? 'Will' then . . . I'm so glad you're here. I was so nervous when I came in here, but you've taken it all away and I'm enjoying just sitting here with you." In her relief at finding a friend, she forgot for a moment their last night together in the hospital and his embrace.

"What about your friend?"

"I never dreamed he'd stand me up, but I really don't care now. It seems right somehow, sitting here with you." Then she blushed. As she said that, he gave her his dazzling smile.

"Would you do me a favor then?"

"What?" She couldn't imagine what favor she could do for him.

"Would you take off that silly wig. I keep thinking I'm talking to Jan."

"You really don't like it?"

"It's not the Jeanine I came to know and . . . in the hospital." She began to giggle.

"To tell you the truth, it was beginning to make my head itch. And, Will, would you mind too much if I slipped off my sandals. My feet are killing me." He chuckled.

"Not a bit. Anything to make you feel more comfortable."

"You know," she spoke between bites, "I'm kind of glad my friend didn't show up. I'm enjoying this salad. I don't believe I could have eaten a bite with him. I feel so comfortable with you . . . like I can be myself and not have to pretend to be a glamourpuss, which I know now, I'm not."

"Oh, Jeanine, Jeanine, you are really something else." He said it softly. "I really should order you a dinner. I don't feel right about you not having a meal."

"I couldn't eat it anyway. My stomach's still churning."

"You mean meeting this friend got you tied up in knots?" Before she realized it, she was telling Will all about Dr. Ben, without mentioning his name.

"Well, you see, I've been writing to him for over six months and I loved his letters, but he might have thought I was a man because I always signed my letters, 'B.J. Pagett.' My Dad wanted a boy, so he named me Billie Jeanine, but called me 'B.J.' After he died, Jan suggested I drop the 'Billie' and just use Jeanine. Dad had this thing about all of us having names that started with a 'J.' I don't know why, he just did." She paused and sipped some tea, but Will just looked at her with his clear, brown eyes.

"I liked Jeanine so much and felt more like a girl. I don't know why I signed my name 'Pagett.' Then," she paused, not knowing if she should continue or not, but then he was a psychiatrist, maybe he could explain her feelings.

"Could I have some more tea, please?" He motioned for a waiter and ordered the tea.

"Then?" he prodded.

"Then I fell in love with him. I didn't even know who he was or what he looked like . . . just a doctor who wrote a column in the newspaper every week. Can you explain that to me? How could one fall in love with a person who just writes letters? But I liked what he wrote and felt I'd like him too. Then I stopped writing because of how I felt. After a month I got this letter from him asking if he'd done something to hurt my feelings and if that's why I'd quit writing. I finally did write to explain about the operation because I wanted him to know about the Lord. I felt it would help him be a better doctor. Then he wrote and said we should meet and asked me to meet him here at 7:00. I guess he didn't want to meet me after all."

"He could have gotten here early and thought you'd stood him up. After all I noticed you were a little later than 7:00."

"We did get tied up in traffic, but he could have waited, if he was that anxious to meet me."

"Yes, he could have and he should have." She felt so relaxed without the wig and the sandals and Will was so easy to talk to . . . just like at the hospital. No! She wouldn't remember the last time she saw him in the hospital.

"Did you ever finish reading *Wuthering Heights?*"

"No. I lost interest."

They talked about life on the river, the places she, Jan and Tommy had been, the things he liked, the things she liked, and she laughed at his wit. She told him about Jan's and her greeting card line and especially the "Cherubs" line.

She looked at her watch. "Oh, my goodness!" she exclaimed and reached under the table, put her sandals back on, grabbed her wig, shawl and purse and started to get up.

"Where are you going?" he asked.

"Jan and Tommy said they'd be back to meet me at 9:30. It's almost that time now. Thank you so much, Will, for a very relaxing evening."

She turned her back to leave when he said softly, "Don't go, Ladybug." She stopped dead still, then slowly turned to him. He had taken off the dark glasses and their eyes locked. Her heart began to betray her by knocking against her ribs. She sat down with her arms hanging down on either side because she became too weak to stand. Her wig drug on the floor on one side and her purse and shawl on the other.

"*You* are Dr. Ben?" She gasped and dropped her things on the floor, grasping the sides of the table to steady her trembling hands. He took one of her hands in his as he nodded. Then he explained. "I didn't know 'B.J.' was a woman at first. Then Tommy kept talking about the family across the river. One day he said, 'You know that boy over there turned out to be a young woman? Her Dad named her Billie Jeanine, but called her 'B.J.' Jeanine, I really treasured every letter you wrote. I got Tommy to describe you to me so I could picture you as I read your letters and knowing that made them mean more to me. But never in all my wildest dreams could I ever have imagined what a lovely young woman you are."

"Why didn't you ever come over with Tommy?"

"I always get home so late and then I didn't want to spoil what we had going in the letters." He was caressing her fingers as he talked.

"But where does Dr. Ben come in?" Jeanine asked.

"My name is William Bennett Rensalear. When mother married Tommy's Dad, he wanted to adopt me, but my mother wanted me to keep the Rensalear name. After she died I had the Bennett name put in my name for Dad's sake. I don't like publicity, so when the newspaper asked me to write a column, I asked them not to put my picture with the column and just called myself, Dr. Ben."

"But I've bared my heart to you. What must you think of me?" Jeanine lowered her eyes and a curl fell onto her forehead. He took his free hand and lifted the curl back into place, then placed his fingers under her chin and raised her face so she had to look at him. Then he spoke softly, ardently, "Just what I thought back in the hospital. Just what I've thought for a long time. Jeanine, I love you, have loved you even before I met you in the hospital. Like you, I fell in love with the writer of those letters, and from all the things Tommy told me. I couldn't hear enough about you."

Her eyes opened wide as she recalled her night in Intensive Care and exclaimed, "You were the one who held my hand in Intensive Care and stayed with me. You told me I'd be fine and called me 'Ladybug'?" He nodded, kissing her fingers, nuzzling them with his lips.

"You were so tiny in that bed and there were all those tubes and stitches and that vapor that had to keep your 'trach' moist. I could hardly stand to see you there. I just couldn't believe you'd make it."

"How did you know I was there?"

"I'm a doctor, remember. When Tommy told me you had

gone to the hospital, I made sure I found out where you were. I kept track of the operation all day. It was five nerve-wracking hours for me. When I finished making my rounds, I saw Jan and Tommy in the Intensive Care lounge and they told me what room you were in. I told them to go home, that I'd be there all night. Being a doctor I could be with you as long as I wanted to."

"In your first letter you called me a 'Ladybug' and I should come out of my cocoon and see what the world is like, yet in Intensive Care and just now you called me 'Ladybug.' Do you still think the same?"

"No, my darling. Now I call you 'Ladybug' because of those cute freckles across your nose. Like a Ladybug's pretty spots, they make you all the more attractive to me. I want to kiss each one. Jeanine, do you think you could love me as Will Rensalear and not Dr. Ben?"

Her eyes sparkled and she gave him her most charming smile.

"I already started to fall for you in the hospital and besides they are the same person are they not? I'm so glad I don't have to choose between them. I love them both."

They looked at each other, their eyes conveying their love one for the other. Then Jeanine sighed and giggled. "Do you suppose we could do something about this mutual feeling we have, Will . . . Dr. Ben?"

"I had the same idea," he exclaimed, laughing that wonderful, deep laugh she loved. He motioned for the waiter to bring his bill and as soon as he appeared, put a bunch of bills on the tray. She picked up her things, he grabbed her hand and led her out very decorously until they got outside. Then he pulled her after him as they ran to his Mercedes. He unlocked the door, opened it and threw her things in the back seat, then turned and opened his arms wide. She ran into them eagerly, her heart doing strange things. He held her in a loving bear hug, twirling her around. "You've made me the happiest man in the world tonight. Oh, Jeanine, how many times in the hospital I wanted to take you in my arms like this and that last night I wanted to keep holding you."

"But you left me. Why did you?"

"Your faith was so strong and I'm just a babe in Christ. I didn't think I was worthy of you. Then I saw the question in your eyes and thought you didn't love me. It's a miracle that you are even here."

"But my faith was made stronger by Dr. Ben."

"What do you mean?"

"One of the reasons I started writing was because I felt Dr. Ben would be a better doctor if he only knew the Lord, so he could pray for his patients. I asked the Lord to let me be a witness to Dr. Ben. Then when I got the cancer I thought that was God's answer to my prayer."

"I still don't understand."

"You see. I felt God was allowing me to have the cancer so when I got well Dr. Ben would know it had to be God doing it through the doctors. That's why I never was afraid." Will smiled, holding her out a little from him.

"Well, it worked. Dr. Ben accepted your Lord. But how was Dr. Ben to get this message?" He asked with a mischievious grin.

"Well, I did write you about it, but you know what happened? Just like Cinderella, my pumpkin coach, Dr. Ben to you, turned into a handsome prince named Will, and here I am. But I cried myself to sleep that last night in the hospital when you didn't come." Will held her close and kissed both her eyes.

"There. Is that better?"

"No. I don't want your kisses on my eyes."

"So, just a few inches down, right?" As their lips met to seal their love and yearning, Will saw the tears glistening on her thick lashes.

"Jeanine are you crying?"

"Yes, but please don't stop kissing me. Those are tears of pure joy. Your 'Ladybug' has found her home."

Epilogue

Jeanine was right. God was not going to leave her without her lower teeth. Two years later, Dr. Goldstein gave permission for Jeanine, now Mrs. Will Rensalear, to have her gum operation.

As soon as she was well and sufficient time had elapsed, according to her orthodontist, she went back to the dentist.

"Here I am," she smiled with a big smile. "I have my new gums and now I'm ready to get my teeth."

The dentist examined her mouth and praised the good job the orthodontist had done, but he surprised her by saying, "I've never made teeth for this kind of situation before. It will be an expensive risk."

Believing firmly that the Lord wasn't through with her until she had some teeth, she stated with conviction, "It will not be a risk. I want you to make the teeth."

And so he did and she is still wearing them to this day.